MW00508897

BIRD OF PARADISE

by the same author

The Twelfth Hour (1907)

Love's Shadow (1908)

The Limit (1911)

Tenterhooks (1912)

Bird of Paradise (1914)

Love at Second Sight (1916)

Letters to the Sphinx from Oscar Wilde
with Reminiscences of the Author (1930)

BIRD OF PARADISE

by

ADA LEVERSON

SANDNESS
MICHAEL WALMER
2022

Bird of Paradise first published 1914
This edition published 2022

by

Michael Walmer
North House
Melby
Sandness
Shetland ZE2 9PL

ISBN 978-0-6452440-8-3 paperback

ERRATA

This edition has been prepared utilizing a previous edition; thus errors have been reproduced. On page 106, line 8, for *then* please read *than*; on page 118, line 18, for *caro* please read *car.*; on page 307, line 8, for *suspicious* please read *suspicions.*

TO

ERNEST

CONTENTS

CHAPTER I

EXCUSES

POOR Madeline came into the room a little flustered and hustled, with papers in her muff. She found Bertha looking lovely and serene as usual.

Madeline Irwin was a modern-looking girl of twenty-three; tall, thin, smart and just the right shape; not pretty, but very sympathetic, with thick dark hair and strongly marked eyebrows, a rather long and narrow face, delicately modelled, a clear white complexion, and soft, sincere brown eyes.

Bertha—Mrs. Percy Kellynch—was known as a beauty. She was indeed improbably pretty, small, plump and very fair, with soft golden hair that was silky and yet fluffy, perfectly regular little features, and a kind of infantine sweetness, combined with an almost incredible cleverness that was curious and fascinating. She was of a type remote equally from the fashion-plate and the suffragette, and was so physically attractive that one could hardly be near her without longing to put out a finger and touch her soft, fair face or her soft hair; as one would like to touch a kitten or a pretty child. And yet one felt that it would not be an entirely safe thing to do; like the child or the kitten she might scratch or run away. But it is probable that a large average of her acquaintance had been weak enough—or strong enough—to give way to the temptation and take the risk.

This charming little creature sat in a room furnished in clear, pale colours—that was pink, white and blonde like herself. Madeline sat down without greeting her, saying in a scolding voice, as she rustled a letter:

"He's refused again . . . more excuses . . . always, always excuses!"

"Well, all the better; excuses are a form of compliment. I'd far rather have a lot of apology and attenuation than utter coolness," said Bertha consolingly. She had a low, even voice, and rarely made a gesture. Her animation was all in her eyes. They were long, bluish-grey, with dark lashes, and very expressive.

"Oh, you'd *like* a man to write and say that he couldn't come to dinner because it was his mother's birthday, and he always dined with her on that occasion, and besides he was in deep mourning, and had influenza, and was going to the first night at the St. James's, and was expecting some old friends up from the country to stay with him, and would be out of town shooting at the time?"

"Certainly; so much inventive ingenuity is most flattering. Don't you think it's better than to say on the telephone that he wouldn't be able to come that evening as he wouldn't be able to; and then ring off?" said Bertha.

"Rupert would never do that! He's intensely polite; politeness is ingrained in his nature. I'm rather hopeless about it all; and yet when I think how sometimes when I speak to him and he doesn't answer but gives that slight smile . . ."

"How well I know that slight, superior smile—discouraging yet spurring you on to further efforts! . . . Rupert—Rupert! What a name! How can people be called Rupert? It isn't done, you're not living in a *feuilleton*, you must change the man's name, dear."

"Indeed I sha'n't! Nonsense; it's a beautiful name! Rupert Denison! It suits him; it suits me. Bertha, you can't deny it's a handsome, noble face, like a Vandyke portrait of Charles I, or one of those people in the National Gallery. And he must take a certain amount of interest in me, because he wants me to learn more, to be more cultured. He's so accomplished! He knows simply everything. The other day he sent me a book about the early Italian masters."

"Did he, though? How jolly!"

"A little volume of Browning, too—that tiny edition, beautifully bound."

Bertha made an inarticulate sound.

"And you know he found out my birthday, and sent me a few dark red roses and Ruskin's Stones of Venice."

"Nothing like being up to date," said Bertha. "Right up to the day after to-morrow! Rupert always is. How did he find out your birthday?"

"How do you suppose?"

"I can't think. By looking in *Who's Who?* —going to Somerset House or the British Museum?"

"How unkind you are! Of course not. No—I told him."

"Ah, I thought perhaps it was some ingenious plan like that. I should think that's the way he usually finds out things—by being told."

"Bertha, why do you sneer at him?"

"Did I?—I didn't mean to. Why does he behave like a belated schoolmaster?"

"Behave like a—oh, Bertha!"

Madeline was trying to be offended, but she could not succeed. It was nearly impossible to be angry with Bertha, when she was present.

There were many reasons for this. Bertha had a small arched mouth, teeth that were tiny and white and marvellously regular, a dimple in her left cheek, long eyelashes that gave a veiled look to the eyes, and a generally very live-wax-dollish appearance which was exceedingly disarming. There was a touch, too, of the china shepherdess about her. But, of course, she was not really like a doll, nor remote from life; she was very real, living and animated; though she had for the connoisseur all the charm of an exquisite *bibelot* that is not for sale.

Bertha was twenty-eight, but looked younger than her age. Madeline might have been her senior. Under this peachlike appearance, and with the premeditated *naïveté* of her manner, she was always astonishing people by her penetration and general ingenuity; she was at once very quick and very deep—quick especially to perceive and enjoy incongruities, and deep in understanding them; extremely observant, and not in the least superficial. Almost her greatest interest was the study of character; she had an intellectual passion for going below the surface, and finding out the little *coins inédits* of the soul. She was rather unpractical, but only in execution, and she had the gift of getting the practical side of life well done for her, not letting it be neglected. Her bonbonnière of a drawing-room seemed to be different from ordinary rooms, though one hardly knew in what; partly from the absence of superfluities; and somehow after many a triumph over the bewilderment of a sulky yet dazzled decorator, Bertha had contrived, in baffling him, to make the house look distinguished without being unconventional; dainty without being artificial; she had made it suit her perfectly and, what was more, the atmosphere was reposeful. Her husband always besought her to do anything on earth she wished in her own home, rather in the same way that one would give an intelligent canary *carte blanche* about the decoration of what was supposed to be its cage.

Percy Kellynch, the husband—he was spoken of as the husband (people said: "Is that the husband?" or "What's the husband like?")—was a rather serious-looking barrister with parliamentary ambitions, two mild hobbies (which took the form of Tschaikowsky at the Queen's Hall and squash rackets at the Bath Club), a fine forehead, behind which there was less doing than one would suppose, polished manners, an amiable disposition and private means.

For Madeline's sake, Bertha was interested in Rupert Denison, and determined to understand him. When she reached bedrock in her friends, it was not unusual for her to grow tired of them. But she was gentle and considerate even to the people who left her cold; and when she really cared for anyone, she was loyal, passionate and extraordinarily tenacious.

"A schoolmaster!" repeated Madeline rather dismally. "Well! perhaps there may be just a touch of that in Rupert. When I'm going to see him I do feel rather nervous and a little as if I was going up for an exam."

"Well, let's say a holiday tutor," conceded Bertha. "He *is* so educational!"

"At any rate, he bothers about what I ought and oughtn't to know; he pays me *some* attention!"

"The only modern thing about him is his paying you so little," said Bertha. "And, Madeline, we mustn't forget that young men are very difficult to get hold of nowadays—for girls. Everyone complains of it. Formerly they wouldn't dance, but they'd do everything else. Now, dancing's the only thing they will do. People are always making bitter remarks to me about it. There's not the slightest doubt that, except for dancing, young men just now, somehow or other, are scarce, wild and shy. And the funny thing is that they'll two-step and one-step and double-Boston and Tango the whole evening, but that's practically all. Oh, they're most unsatisfactory! Lots of girls have told me so. And as to proposals! Why, they're the *rarest* thing! Even when the modern young man is devoted you can't be sure of serious intentions, except, of course, in the Royal Family, or at the Gaiety."

"Well, *I* don't care! I'm sure I don't want all these silly dancing young men. They bore me to death. Give me *culture*! and all that sort of thing. Only—only Rupert! . . . Very often after he's refused an invitation, like this of mother's, he'll write and ask me to have tea with him at Rumpelmeyer's, or somewhere; and then he'll talk and talk the whole time about . . . oh, any general instructive subject."

"For instance?"

"Oh . . . architecture!"

"How inspiriting!"

"But does it all mean anything, Bertha?"

"I almost think it must," she answered dreamily. "No man could take a girl out to eat ices and talk of the cathedral at Rouen, or discuss Pointed Gothic and Norman arches over tea and bread and butter, without *some* intentions. It wouldn't be human."

"It's quite true he always seems to take a good deal for granted," remarked Madeline. "But not enough."

"Exactly!"

"Rupert would make a very good husband—if you could stand him," said Bertha meditatively; "he's one of those thoroughly well-informed people who never know what is going on."

"If I could *stand* him! Why, Bertha! I'd work my fingers to the bone, and lay down my life for him!"

"He doesn't want your life, and, probably, not bony fingers either, but he'll want incense swung, *all* the time, remember; and always in front of him only. He won't be half as good-natured and indulgent as Percy."

"Of course, Percy's very sweet, and kind and clever, and devoted to you," said Madeline, "but I always feel that it would have been more your ideal to have married your first love, Nigel; and far more romantic, too. He's so good-looking and amusing, and how delightfully he sings Debussy!"

"Nigel! Oh, nonsense. There's no one more really prosaic. Debussy, indeed! I met him with his wife the other night at the opera and he introduced us. My dear, she's got flat red hair, an aigrette, a turned-up nose, a receding chin and long ear-rings; and she's quite young and very dowdy: the sort of dowdiness that's rather smart. She loathed me—that is to say, we took a mutual dislike, and a determination never to meet again, so strong that it amounted to a kind of friendship; we tacitly agreed to keep out of each other's way. I suppose there's such a thing as a sort of comradeship in aversion," Bertha added thoughtfully.

"Oh, Bertha, fancy anybody disliking you!"

"It's only because Nigel had told her, *in camera*, that he was in love with me once, and that we were almost engaged."

"Did he say who broke it off?"

"Yes, I should think he told the truth—that he did—but he didn't mention the real reasons, that he was horribly hard up and saw a chance of marrying an heiress. I daresay, too, that he said no other woman would ever be quite the same to him again, for fear Mrs. Nigel should be too pleased. Nigel is nice and amusing and he's sometimes very useful. He thinks he treated me badly, and really has got to appreciate me since, and as he knows I'm utterly indifferent to him now, he's devoted, I mean as a friend—he'll do anything on earth for me. He has absolutely nothing to do, you see; it's a kindness to employ him."

"What do you give him to do?"

"It depends. This time I've told him to get hold of Rupert and ask us all three—I mean you, and me and Rupert—to dine and go to some play. It would be so much less ceremonious than asking Rupert here, with Percy."

"Oh, darling Bertha, you're an angel! I always said Nigel was charming. What about Mrs. Nigel, and Percy?"

"Don't worry; that shall be arranged. Their rights shall not be ignored, nor their interests neglected! Percy's little finger is worth all Nigel. Still, Nigel has his good points; he might help us in this. There are so many things he can do, he's so *fin*—and adaptable, and diplomatic. That young brother of his, Charlie, is in love with you, Madeline. Now, he's a boy who *could* marry, and who wants to. If you gave him only a look of encouragement he would propose at once. And he has a good deal of Nigel's charm, though he's not so clever, but he's very much steadier. Really, it's a pity you don't like him. I'm sorry."

"Oh, I couldn't," said Madeline.

"He's quite a nice boy, too; and I know how much he likes you, from Nigel."

"Oh, I couldn't!" Madeline repeated, shaking her head.

Bertha seemed silently to assent.

"And will dear Nigel ask me all the same to meet Rupert, Bertha?"

"Oh yes; we'll arrange it to-day. Nigel's delightfully prompt, and never delays anything."

"And what will happen to Percy? You scarcely ever go out without him."

"Oh, I can persuade Percy, for once, that he wants his mother to go with him to the Queen's Hall. And I'll make Lady Kellynch think it's rather a shame of her to take my place; then she'll enjoy it. We'll arrange it for next week. I'm expecting her this afternoon."

"Oh, are you? I'm always rather afraid she doesn't like me," said Madeline pensively.

"She doesn't *dis*like you. She doesn't dislike anybody; only, simply, you don't exist for her. My mother-in-law really believes that the whole of humanity consists of her own family; first, her late husband; then Percy, then Clifford, the boy at school, and, in a very slight degree, me too, because I'm married to Percy. I do like Clifford, though he's a spoilt boy, and selfish. But he's great fun. How his mother adores him! I hope she won't stay long to-day —Nigel will be here at six."

Madeline fell into a reverie, a sort of mental swoon. Then she suddenly woke up and said with great animation,—

"No, I suppose I dare not hope it!—I believe I should expire with joy!—but he *never* will! But if he *did* propose, how do you suppose he'd do it, Bertha?"

"Heaven knows—quote Browning, I suppose," said Bertha, "I don't often meet that type. I can only guess. Do you care so much, Madeline?"

"*Do* I care!"

"And you believe it's the real thing?"

"I know it is—on my side; it's incurable."

"Everyone says Rupert's a good fellow, but he seems to me a little—what shall I say?—too elaborate. Too urbane; too ornate. He expresses himself so dreadfully well! I don't believe he ever uses a shorter word than *individuality*!"

"Oh, I don't care what he is, I want him—I want him!" cried Madeline.

"Well! I suppose you know what you want. It isn't as though you were always in love with somebody or other; as a rule, a girl of your age, if she can't have the person she wants, can be very quickly consoled if you give her someone else instead. Now, you've never had even a fancy before. *I* may not (I don't) see the charm of Rupert, but it must be there; probably there's something in his temperament that's needed by yours—something that he can supply to you that no one else can. If you really want him, you must have him, darling," said Bertha, with resolution. "You shall!"

"How can you say that; how can you make him care for me if he doesn't?"

"I don't know, but I shall. It's certain; don't worry; and do what I tell you. Mind, I think that there are many other people far more amusing, besides being better matches from the worldly point of view—like Charlie Hillier, for instance—but the great thing is that you care for your Rupert; and I don't believe you'll change."

They were never demonstrative to each other, and Madeline only looked at her with trusting, beaming gratitude. Bertha was indeed convinced that this mania for Rupert was the real thing; it would never fade from fulfilment, nor even die if discouraged; it would always burn unalterably bright.

"Yes; yes, it shall be all right," repeated Bertha.

She spoke in a curious, reassuring tone that Madeline knew, and that always impressed her.

"Really? Yet you say they are so difficult nowadays!"

"Well, the majority of the men in our set certainly don't seem to be exactly pining for hearth and home. Still, in some moods a man will marry anyone who happens to be there."

"Then must I happen to be there? How can I?"

Bertha laughed. There was a confidence without reservation between them, notwithstanding a slight tinge of the histrionic in Madeline, which occasionally irritated Bertha. But the real link was that they both instinctively threw overboard all but the essential; they cared comparatively little for most of the preoccupations and smaller solicitudes of the women in their own leisured class. There was in neither of them anything of the social snob or the narrow outlook of the bourgeoise; they were free from pose, petty ambitions, or trivial affectations.

Madeline looked up to Bertha as a wonderful combination of kindness, cleverness, beauty and knowledge of the world. Bertha felt that Madeline was not quite so well equipped for dealing with life as she herself was; there was a shade of protection in her friendship.

Bertha was far more daring than Madeline, but her occasional recklessness was only pluck and love of adventure; not imprudence; it was always guided by reason and an instinctive sense of self-preservation. She was a little experimental, that was all. Madeline was more timid and sensitive; though not nearly so quick to see things as Bertha she took them to heart more, far more;—was far less lively and ironical.

"Though I find Rupert dull, as I say, I believe he's as good as gold, or I wouldn't try and help you. Now if he were a man like Nigel!—who's very much more fascinating and charming—I wouldn't raise a finger, because I know he's fickle, dangerous and selfish, and wouldn't make you happy. Charlie would, though; I wish you liked Charlie. But one can't account for these things."

"Quite impossible," Madeline said, shaking her head.

"Well! It's quite possible that Rupert would suit you best; and I believe if you once got him he'd be all right. And you shall!" she repeated.

"*Thank* you!" said Madeline fervently, as if Bertha had promised her a box of chocolates or a present of some kind.

"Lady Kellynch!" announced the servant.

CHAPTER II

LADY KELLYNCH

A TALL, stately, handsome woman, slow and quiet in movement, dressed in velvet and furs, came deliberately into the room. The magnificent, imposing Lady Kellynch had that quiet dignity and natural ease and distinction sometimes seen in the widow of a knight, but unknown amongst the old aristocracy. It was generally supposed, or, at all events, stated, that the late Sir Percy Kellynch had been knighted by mistake for somebody else; through a muddle owing to somebody's deafness. The result was the same, since his demise left her with a handle to her name, but no one to turn it (to quote the *mot* of a well-known wit), and she looked, at the very least, like a peeress in her own right. Indeed, she was the incarnation of what the romantic lower middle classes imagine a great lady;—a dressmaker's ideal of a duchess. She had the same high forehead, without much thought behind it, so noticeable in her son Percy, and the same clearly cut features; and it was true, as Bertha had said, that she firmly believed the whole of the world, of the slightest importance, consisted of her late husband, herself, her married son Percy, and her boy Clifford at school; the rest of the universe was merely an audience, or a background, for this unique family.

If anyone spoke of a European crisis that was interesting the general public, she would reply by saying what Percy thought about it; if a more frivolous subject (such as *You Shut Up*, or some other popular Revue) was mentioned, she would answer, reassuringly, that she knew Clifford had a picture post-card of one of the performers, implying thereby that it *must* be all right. She loved Bertha mildly, and with reservations, because Percy loved her, and because Bertha wished her to; but she really thought it would have been more suitable if Bertha had been a little more colourless, a little plainer, a little stupider and more ordinary; not that her attractions would ever cause any trouble to Percy, but because it seemed as if a son of hers ought to have a wife to throw him up more. Percy, however, had no idea that Bertha was anything but a good foil to him, intellectually—and, as I have said, he regarded her (or believed he regarded her) a good deal like a pet canary.

"Percy will soon be home, I suppose? To-day is not the day he goes to the Queen's Hall, is it?" asked Lady Kellynch, who thought any hall was highly honoured by Percy's presence, and very lucky to get it. She gave a graceful but rather unrecognising bow to Madeline, whom she never knew by sight. She really knew hardly anyone by sight except her sons; and this was the more odd as she had a particularly large circle of acquaintances, and made a point of accepting and returning every invitation she received, invariably being amongst those present at every possible form of entertainment, and punctiliously calling on people afterwards. She was always mounting staircases, going up in lifts, and driving about leaving cards, and was extremely hospitable and superlatively social. Bertha always wondered at her gregariousness, since one would fancy she could have got very little satisfaction in continual intercourse with a crowd of people whom she forgot the instant they were out of her sight. Lady Kellynch really knew people chiefly by their telephone numbers and their days, when they had any. She would say: "Mrs. So-and-so? Oh yes, six-three-seven-five Gerrard, at home on Sundays," but could rarely recollect anything else about her. She was at once vague and precise, quite amiable, very sentimental and utterly heartless; except to her sons.

"No, Percy won't be home till dinner-time. To-day he's playing squash rackets."

"That's so like his father," said Lady Kellynch admiringly. "He was always so fond of sports, and devoted to music. When I say sports, to be *strictly* accurate I don't mean that he ever cared for rude, rough games like football or anything cruel like hunting or shooting, but he loved to look on at a game of cricket, and I've often been to Lord's with him." She sighed. "Dominoes! he was wild about dominoes! I assure you (dear Percy would remember), every evening after dinner he must have his game of dominoes, and sometimes even after lunch."

"Dominoes, as you say, isn't exactly a field sport," sympathetically agreed Bertha.

"Quite so, dear. But, however, that was his favourite game. Then, did I say just now he was fond of music? He didn't care for the kind that Percy likes, but he would rarely send a piano-organ away, and he even encouraged the German bands. How fond he was of books too—and reading, and that sort of thing!

Percy gets his fondness for books from his father. Clifford too is fond of books."

"He is indeed," said Bertha; "he's devoted to books. Last time I went to see him, when he was at home for the holidays, I found among his books a nice copy of 'The New Arabian Nights.' We hadn't one in the house at the time, and I asked him to lend it to me."

"Did you indeed?"

Lady Kellynch looked a shade surprised, as if it had been rather a liberty.

"Well," said Bertha, laughing, and turning to Madeline, "what do you think he said? 'Bertha, I'm awfully sorry, but I make it a rule never to lend books. I don't approve of it—half the time they don't come back, and in fact—oh, I don't think it's a good plan. I never do it.' I took up the book and found written in it: '*To Bertha, with love from Percy.*' I said: 'So you don't approve of lending books. Do you see this is my book?' He looked at it and said solemnly: 'Yes, so it is, but I can't let you have it. I'm in the middle of it. Besides—oh! anyhow, I want it!'"

Madeline and Bertha both laughed, saying that Clifford was really magnificent for twelve years old.

Lady Kellynch seemed astonished at their amusement. She only said: "Oh yes; I know Clifford's *most* particular about his books."

"And even about my books," said Bertha.

"Quite so, dear. They say in his report that he's getting so orderly. It's a very good report this term—er—at least, very good on the *whole.*"

"Oh, do let me see it."

"No, I don't think I'll show it you. But I'll tell you what I'll do, I'll read you some extracts from it, if you like." She said this as if it were an epic poem, and she was promising them a rare literary treat.

She took something out of her bag. "I know he doesn't work *very* hard at school, but then the winter term is such a trying one; so cold for them to get up in the morning, poor little darlings!"

"Poor pets!" said Bertha.

Lady Kellynch took it out, while the others looked away discreetly, as she searched for suitable selections.

After a rather long pause she read aloud, a little pompously and with careful elocution: "'*Doing fairly well in dictation, and becoming more accurate; in Latin moderate, scarcely up to the level of the form. . . .*'"

"Is it in blank verse?" asked Bertha.

"Oh no! . . . Of course he's in a very high form for his age." She then went on, after a longer pause: "'*Music and dancing: music, rather weak . . . dancing, a steady worker.*' That's very good, isn't it? . . . '*Map-drawing: very slovenly.*'" (She read this rather proudly.) "'*Conduct: lethargic and unsteady; but a fair speller.*' Excellent, isn't it? Of course they're frightfully severe at that school. . . . Oh yes, and there's '*Bible good, but deficient in general knowledge. Has a little ability, but rarely uses it. . . .*' It's dreadfully difficult to please them, really! But I think it's very satisfactory, don't you?"

Realising that Lady Kellynch had only read aloud the very best and most brilliant extracts that she could find in the report—purple patches, as one may say—Bertha gathered that it could hardly have been worse. So she congratulated the mother warmly and cordially, and said how fond she was of Clifford.

"He will be home soon for the Easter holidays. You must let him come and stay with us."

"It's very kind of you, dear. Certainly he shall come, part of the time. I can't bear to part with him—especially at first. Yes—at first I feel I never want him to leave me again! However, he enjoys himself so much here that I like to send him to you towards the end. He looks upon Bertha quite like a playmate," she said to Madeline. Something about Madeline reminded her of someone she had met.

"I was at a dinner-party last night where I met a young man I saw here once, who took you in to dinner. He knows Percy—he was at Balliol with Percy—a Mr. Denison—Mr. Rupert Denison. He seemed inclined to be rather intellectual. He talked to me a great deal about something—I forget what; but I know it was some subject: something that Percy once had to pass an examination in. . . . I can't remember what it was. I used to know his mother; Mrs. Denison—a charming woman! I'm afraid though she didn't leave him very well off. I wonder how he manages to make two ends meet?"

"He manages all right; he makes them lap over, I should think. Who did he take to dinner?" Bertha asked this in Madeline's interest.

"Oh, a girl I don't like at all, whom I often see about. She's always everywhere. I daresay you know her, a Miss Chivvey, a Miss Moona Chivvey—a good family, the Chivveys of Warwickshire. But she's rather artistic-looking." (Lady Kellynch lowered her voice as if she were saying something improper:) "She has untidy hair and green beads round her neck. I don't like her—I don't like her style at all."

"I've heard him mention her," said Madeline.

"He talked to her a good deal in the evening, and he gave me the impression that he was giving her some sort of lesson—a lecture on architecture, or something. Well, dear, as Percy won't be in yet, I think I'd better go. I have a round of visits to pay."

"Percy is going to write to you. He wants you to go to a concert with him. He particularly wants you to go."

Lady Kellynch brightened up. "Dear boy, does he? Of course I'll go. Well, good-bye, darling."

She swept from the room with the queenly grace and dignity that always seemed a little out of proportion to the occasion—one expected her to make a court curtsy, and go out backwards.

"My mother-in-law really believes it matters whether she calls on people or not," said Bertha, in her low, even voice. "Isn't it touching?"

Madeline seized her hand.

"Bertha, need I be frightened of Moona Chivvey? She's a dangerous sort of girl; she takes interest in all the things Rupert does: pictures, and poetry and art needlework."

"Does Rupert really do art needlework? What a universal genius he is!"

"Don't be absurd! I mean the things he understands. And she runs after him, rather. Need I be afraid?"

"No, you need not," reassured Bertha. "I don't think she sounds at all violent. There's a ring."

"Then I'll go."

Almost immediately afterwards the servant announced "Mr. Nigel Hillier."

Nigel Hillier came in cheerily and gaily, brimming over with vitality and in the highest spirits. At present he was like sunshine and fresh air. There was a lurking danger that as he grew older he might become breezy. But as yet there was no sign of a draught. He was just delightfully exhilarating. He was not what women call handsome or divine, but he was rather what men call a smart-looking chap: fair, with bright blue eyes, and the most mischievous smile in London. He was unusually rapid in thought, speech and movement, without being restless, and his presence was an excellent cure for slackness, languor, strenuousness or a morbid sense of duty.

"You look as if you had only just got up," remarked Bertha, as she gave him her hand. "Not a bit as though you'd been through the fatigues and worries and the heat and burden of the day."

"Oh, that's too bad!" he answered. "You know perfectly well I always get up in time to see the glorious sunset! Why this reproach? I don't know that I've ever seen you very early in the day; I always regard you less as a daughter of the morning than as a minion of the moon."

"How is Mrs. Hillier?" replied Bertha rather coldly.

"All right—I promise I won't. Mary? Why Mary is well—very well—but just, perhaps, a teeny bit trying—just a shade wearing. No—no, I don't mean that. . . . Well, I'm at your service for the play and so on. Shall I write to Rupert Denison and Miss Irwin? And will you all come and dine with me, and where shall we go?"

"Don't you think something thrilling and exciting and emotional—or, perhaps, something light and frivolous?"

"For Rupert I advise certainly the trivial, the flippant. It would have a better effect. Why not go to the new Revue—'*That will be Fourpence*'—where they have the two young Simultaneous Dancers, the Misses Zanie and Lunie Le Face—one, I fancy, is more simultaneous than the other, I forget which. They are delightful, and will wake Denison up. In fact, I don't know who they *wouldn't* wake up, they make such a row. They dance and sing, about Dixie and Honey and coons—and that sort of thing. They sing quite well, too —I mean for them."

"But not for us? . . . No, I don't want to take him with Madeline to anything that could be called a music-hall—something more correct for a *jeune fille* would be better. . . ."

"To lead to a proposal, you mean. Well, we'd better fall back upon His Majesty's or Granville Barker. Poor Charlie! It's hard lines on that boy, Bertha—he's really keen on Miss Irwin."

"I know; but what can we do? It's Rupert Denison she cares about."

"Likes him, does she?" said Nigel.

"Very much," answered Bertha, who rarely used a strong expression, but whose eyes made the words emphatic.

Nigel whistled. "Oh, well, if it's as bad as that!"

"It is. Quite."

"Fancy! Lucky chap, old Rupert. Well, we must rush it through for them, I suppose. About the play—you want something serious, what price Shakespeare?"

"No price. Let's go to the Russian Ballet."

"Capital!" cried Nigel, moving quickly to the telephone in case she should change her mind; "and we'll dine at the Carlton first. May I use your telephone?"

"Please!"

CHAPTER III

NIGEL

THE relation between Bertha and Nigel Hillier was a rather curious one. He had met her when she was eighteen. The attraction had been sudden, violent and mutual; and she was quite prepared to marry him against all opposition. There had been a good deal in her own family, because Nigel was what is euphemistically called without means, and she was the daughter of a fashionable London vicar who, though distinguished for his eloquence and extremely popular, successful and social, had a comparatively small income and a positively large family. In a short time Nigel —not Bertha—succumbed to the family opposition and the general prudent disapproval of worldly friends. He wrote and told Bertha that he was afraid after all they were right; persuaded to this view by having meanwhile met the only daughter of a millionaire when staying for a week-end at a country house.

The girl had fallen in love with him, and was practically independent.

A few months after his gorgeous wedding, described and photographed with the greatest enthusiasm in all the illustrated papers, Bertha married Percy Kellynch, to the great satisfaction of her relations. Nigel was, by then, a lost illusion, a disappointed ideal; she did not long resent his defection and it cured her passion, but she despised him for what she regarded as the baseness of his motive.

She loved and looked up to Percy, but her marriage to him had not been at the time one of romance—to her great regret. She would have liked it to be, for she was one of those ardent souls to whom the glamour of love was everything; she could never worship false gods. But Bertha had a warm, grateful nature, and finding him even better than she expected, her affection threw out roots and tendrils; became deeper and deeper; her experience with Nigel had made her particularly appreciative of Percy's good qualities. She was expansive, affectionate and constant; and she really cared far more about Percy now than she did when she married him. And this, though she was quite aware that he was entirely wanting in several things that she had particularly valued in Nigel (a sense of humour for one), and that he had inherited rather acutely the depressing Kellynch characteristic of taking oneself seriously.

Percy, on the other hand, had been quite carried away by her rosebud charm and prettiness, and he had continued to regard her as a pet and a luxury (for he was pre-eminently one of that large class of people who see only the obvious). But he had never realised her complexities, and was quite unaware of her depth and strength of mind. He was proud of her popularity, and had never known a jealous moment. Since they had never had a shadow of a quarrel, theirs might certainly be described as a happy marriage; although Bertha had always found it from the first rather deficient in the elements of excitement and a little wanting in fun.

Nigel, who had been in a frightful hole when he met the heiress, of course made a point of discovering, as soon as all grinding money troubles had been removed and agonising debts paid, that no material things were capable of making him happy. The gratification to his vanity of his big country house, and charming house in London and so forth, amused him for a very short time. He became horribly bored, and when Bertha married

Percy Kellynch, felt pained and particularly surprised and disappointed in her. He had always believed her to be so superior to other girls, so true and loyal! It was quite a disillusion; to think that she could get over *him* so easily! Women usually took much longer than that. However, he now despised himself even more as a fool than as a coward for having given up Bertha, and not being of the type who trouble to conceal their feelings in domestic life, he openly and frankly showed to the unfortunate Mary that he knew he had made an irrevocable mistake. This was the natural way of regaining his self-respect, since he was under the deepest obligation to her. To add to his annoyance, not long after the marriage he and his brother Charlie came into a legacy from an unexpected and forgotten relative. He knew, then, that if he had waited a little longer, (as she had wished), he could, without sacrifice, have married Bertha; and so he was naturally very angry with Mary.

Now that Bertha was beyond his reach she seemed to him the one desirable thing in the world. For several years they hardly met; then Nigel contrived that they should become friends again. Her feeling for him could never be revived. His was far more vivid than formerly.

It was fanned by her coolness, and was in a fair way to become an *idée fixe*, for he was not material enough to live without some dream, some ideal, and Bertha found him amusing. There always had been a certain mental sympathy between them; in a sense (superficially and humorously), they saw life very much from the same standpoint. With the instinctive tact of the real lover of women he carefully concealed from her the secret that made his home life miserable, instead of merely tedious. It was, simply, that Mary was morbidly, madly jealous of him. He had shown far too soon that he had married her for her money, and if he had convinced her that she had bought him, it was perhaps natural in return that she should wish for her money's worth. The poor woman was passionately in love with Nigel. She suspected him of infidelity, with and without reason, morning, noon, and night; it was almost a monomania. They had two children in the first and second years of the marriage. Nigel was carelessly fond of them, but he regarded them rather as a private luxury and resource of his wife, mistakenly thinking their society could fill up all the gaps made by his rather frequent absences. Nigel knew better than to complain of his wife, or to ask for sympathy from Bertha, for he was certain that if she had the faintest idea of the jealousy, her door would be closed to him.

Bertha was peculiarly kind, peculiarly full of sympathy for her own sex. And yet she was not at all fond of the society of women, with few exceptions; and she was often bored by the liking and admiration she usually inspired in them. Something in her personality disarmed ordinary jealousy, for though she was pretty and attractive, it was easy for other women to see that she was not trying to attract. What the average woman resents in another woman is not her involuntary charm; it is her making use of it.

With the casual indiscretion of the selfish man, Nigel, of course, told his wife at length, early in the honeymoon, all about his romance with Bertha. This Mary had never forgiven. Curiously, she minded more this old innocent affair of ten years ago, which he had broken off for *her*, than any of his flirtations since. Bertha had rightly guessed that, when they met, Mary had taken a great dislike to her. But she had no idea that Nigel's wife was suspicious, nor that she seriously and bitterly resented his visits. He never admitted them to Mary if he could help it, for he had learnt by now to be so far considerate to her—or to himself—that he would tell her fifty fibs in half-an-hour rather than let out one annoying fact. Nigel saw—he was very quick in these matters—that the only terms on which he could ever see anything of Bertha were those of the intimate old brotherly friend; the slightest look or suggestion of sentiment of any kind made her curl up and look angry. She made it utterly impossible for him to make the slightest allusion to the past. The friendliness had been growing to intimacy, and Nigel believed that perhaps with time he might get back to the old terms, or something like them. It was becoming the chief object of his life. He was a keen sportsman, and the ambition of the hunter was added to the longing of the lover. A born diplomatist, he had, of course, easily made Percy like him immensely. But he hated Percy, and could never forgive him for the unpardonable injury he had done to him, Nigel, in consoling Bertha. Nigel could not bear to own, even to himself, that Bertha was happy in her married life. Sometimes he would swear to himself when he remembered that it was all his own doing, that she might have been *his* wife. How coolly she had taken it! She had accepted it at the time with calm acquiescence, and met him again with amiable composure. Had she ever really forgiven him?

It had opened her eyes, had been a shock. She saw him now as the shattered dream of her childish fancy, and she was thankful for her escape. Yet deep down in her heart was a slight scar. It did not make her hate Nigel, but apart from the fun and pleasantness of their intercourse her real indifference to him was slightly tinged with acidity: probably she would have been less sorry for him in any trouble than for anybody else.

Bertha's vanity was not a very vivid part of her, and it took only one form. When she cared for anyone she was deeply (though not outwardly) exacting; she wanted that person entirely. To say that the general admiration she received gave her no pleasure would be an absurd exaggeration; if she had suddenly lost it, she would have missed it very much, no doubt. But after all, she valued it chiefly because she thought it was good for Percy. Privately she was not satisfied that Percy valued her enough. Had her many friends and acquaintances been told that the chief wish of the pretty Mrs. Kellynch was the more complete and absolute conquest of her own husband

—who seemed much more devoted than most husbands—they would have been surprised, incredulous, perhaps even a little shocked.

Nigel had promised to use all the means at his disposal to help Madeline. Bertha was anxious her friend should have what she had just missed.

"Well! Soon after the dinner I shall go and see Rupert in his rooms. I shall get to know him well, and I shall gradually tell him about Charlie, and how keen he is, and lead up to Miss Irwin, and say what a charming girl she is, and all that sort of thing. Nothing makes so much impression."

"Don't make him jealous of Charlie," said Bertha. "Anything that he regarded as a slight I think would put an end to it. Rupert is not quite a commonplace man."

"Jealous? Oh no, I should merely imply that Miss Madeline won't have anything to say to Charlie, and that I wonder why. But it can't do him any harm to know someone else wants her. My dear girl, a man understands another man. That is where women are such fools. They think they know more about men than men do, and that is why they are always being——" He stopped.

She smiled.

"Oh no. I quite do you justice, Nigel. I am never above consulting you on that sort of subject. I may know just a little bit more about men than some women do, for one reason——"

"And what is that? Because you attract them?"

"No, that doesn't help much. It's because I have brothers, and they have always confided in me without reserve. Oh! there was one more thing I *may* have to ask you. I don't want to, and I don't like it at all, on account of Mrs. Hillier; but still it might happen to be necessary. It's *just* possible I may ask you to flirt a little with a girl called Moona Chivvey."

"Oh, *I* know her." He smiled. "Of course I'd do anything for you, but *that* would be about the hardest thing you could command."

"She's not uninteresting," said Bertha. "I shall find out how she stands with Rupert, and I don't think there's much danger. But if it should be required—well—you might go further and fare worse."

"I expect I should go further than Rupert," murmured Nigel.

"Nigel, *don't* think I haven't scruples about things. I have, very much, but I know a good deal about Moona, and I really think that any harmless thing we can do to remove obstacles for poor Madeline should be done. I promised

Madeline. I shall be grateful if you'll help, Nigel."

"There's no question about it," said Nigel. "Of course it must be rushed through. And now I suppose you want me to go?"

"Oh no! Please don't! Percy will be here directly."

He got up.

"Good-bye. I'll ring you up to-morrow. It's some little consolation for being an idle man to have leisure to fulfil your commands."

She answered that he was very good and she was very pleased with him, and he went away.

CHAPTER IV

RUPERT AT RUMPELMEYER'S

AT a quarter to four precisely, in a heavy shower of rain, Madeline sprang out of a taxicab in St. James's Street, and tripped into Rumpelmeyer's. As it was pouring lavishly and she had no umbrella, she hastily and enthusiastically overpaid the cabman, with a feeling of superstition that it might bring her luck; besides, a few drops of rain, she reflected, would ruin her smart new hat if she waited for change. It was a very small hat, over her eyes, decorated with a very high feather, in the form of a lightning-conductor. She was charmingly dressed in a way that made her look very tall, slim and elegant. Her rather long, sweet face was paler than usual, her sincere brown eyes brighter. She had come to have tea with Rupert.

From the back room, waiting for her, rose the worshipped hero. He was, as she had described him, very much like a Vandyke picture. He had broad shoulders, and a thin waist, a pointed brown beard, regular features, very large deep blue eyes, and an absurdly small mouth with dazzling white teeth. If he was almost too well dressed—so well that one turned round to look at his clothes—his distinguished manners and *grand seigneur* air carried it off. One saw it was not the over-dressing of the *nouveau riche*, but the rather old-world dandyism of a past generation. This was the odder as the year was 1913, and he was exactly thirty. He always wore a buttonhole—to-day it was made of violets to match his violet socks—and invariably carried a black ebony stick, with an ivory handle.

With a quiet smile on his small mouth, he greeted and calmed the agitated Madeline.

She dropped her bag on the floor before she sat down, and when Rupert picked it up for her she dropped it again on a plate of cream cakes. He then took it and moved it to his side of the table.

"I thought," he said smoothly, in a rather low, soothing voice, "that you'd like these cakes better than toast."

She eagerly assured him that he was right, though it happened to be quite untrue.

"And China tea, of *course?*"

"Oh, of *course!*" She disliked it particularly.

"And now, tell me, how has life been treating you?" he asked, as he looked first at her, and then with more eager interest at his pointed polished finger-nails.

Before she could answer, he went on:

"And that book on architecture that I sent you—tell me, have you read it?"

"Every word."

This was perfectly true; she could have passed an examination in it.

"That's delightful. Then, now that you know something about it, I should like very much to take you to Westminster Abbey or St. Paul's, or to see one of those really beautiful old cathedrals. . . . We must plan it out."

"Oh, please do. I revel in old things," she said, thinking the remark would please him.

He arranged his buttonhole of Parma violets, then looked up at her, smiling.

"Do you mean that at your age you really appreciate the past?"

"Indeed, I do."

"But you mustn't live for it, you know—not over-value it. You must never forget that, after all, the great charm of the past is that it is over. One must live for the hour, for the moment. . . . You'll remember that, won't you?"

"Oh yes, I *do*," she said gratefully, taking a bite of cream cake.

"What they call Futurism (I hope you understand) is absolute rubbish and inconsistent nonsense. For this reason. It's impossible to enjoy the present or the future if you eliminate the past entirely, as the so-called Futurists wish to do. Destruction of old associations and treasures would ruin one's sense of proportion; it's worse than living in the prehistoric. Besides, at least we know what *has* happened, and what *is* happening, but we can't possibly know what is *going* to be, what the future holds for us; so what's the point of thinking only of that? Why should we live only for posterity, when, as the old joke says, posterity has done nothing for us!"

"Well, the truth is *I* always feel nothing matters except now," said Madeline candidly.

He laughed. "And, in a way, you're right; it's all we're quite sure of."

"Yes, I'm afraid it is."

"By the way," he said, dropping his instructive manner," can you tell me where you get your hats? Do you mind?"

"Oh yes, of course I can; at several places. This one came from——" She hesitated a moment.

"Paquin?" he asked, in a low, mysterious voice.

"Selfridge," she replied.

"Oh, I didn't know you were a Selfridgette! But, please forgive my asking, won't you? Someone who didn't seem to know . . . I mean, a friend of mine. . . . Oh, well, I know you don't mind telling me."

He looked hard at her hat, could find no fault with it. Evidently its value was not diminished in his eyes. He was rather gratified that it did not come from some impossibly costly place. This pleased her; it was a good sign. Satisfaction at a moderate indication of economy suggested serious intentions.

"It suits you very well," he went on, in his kind, approving way. "Now, will you give me another cup of tea?"

She poured it out rather shakily.

"No sugar, please."

"Oh!" She had already nervously dropped in about three lumps.

"Oh well, never mind. . . . Yes, you're looking charming, Madeline—it's absurd calling you Miss Irwin after knowing each other so long, isn't it?"

She was so delighted that she almost thanked him for calling her by her Christian name.

"Do you know, Madeline," he went on, "that, at times, you're almost a beauty."

She opened her mouth with surprise.

"*Almost*. You were one evening—I forget which evening—you had something gold in your hair, and you were quite Byzantine. And then, again, a few days after I saw you, and—er —oh well, anyhow—you always look nice."

"I suppose you mean," she murmured, feeling shy at talking so much of herself, "that most girls look best in the evening."

"There I venture to differ from you entirely. All girls, all women, look their best in the afternoon. The hat is everything. Evening dress is the most trying and unbecoming thing in the world; only the most perfect beauties, who are also very young and fresh, can stand it. The most becoming thing for a woman is either *néqligé*, or a hat. You, particularly, Madeline, look your best in the afternoon."

"I wish then that I lived in that land where it is always afternoon!" she said, laughing.

He gave his superior little smile. "The Lotus Eaters? Good. I didn't know you cared for Tennyson."

"I don't," she answered hastily, anxious to please.

He raised his eyebrows. "Then you should. Have you a favourite poet, Madeline?"

"Oh yes, of course—Swinburne."

She thought this a perfectly safe thing to say.

"Strong meat for babes," he of course replied, and then began to murmur to himself: "*For a day and a night love sang to us, played with us.* You think that beautiful, Madeline?"

"Oh yes. How beautifully you say it!"

He laughed. "Quoting poetry at Rumpelmeyer's! Well, perhaps no place is quite prosaic where . . ."

She looked up.

He took another tea-cake.

. . . "Where there's anyone so interested, so intelligent as yourself."

He had returned to the indulgent, encouraging schoolmaster's tone.

"Do you know In the Orchard?" he went on, and murmured: "*Ah God, ah God! that day should be so soon!* Well! May I smoke a cigarette?"

"Oh, of *course*."

"Oh . . . Madeline!"

"Yes, Mr. Denison?"

"Who is Nigel Hillier?"

"Oh, don't you know him?"

"Of course I know him; we belong to the same club, and that sort of thing, but that doesn't tell me who he is."

She was wondering what Rupert meant exactly by who, but supposed he was speaking socially, so she said hesitatingly:

"Well, Nigel Hillier . . . he married that Miss——"

He interrupted her, putting up his hand rather like a policeman in the traffic. "I know all about his marriage, my dear friend. I didn't ask you whom he married. Who *is* he?"

"Bertha and Percy have known him all their lives—at least all Bertha's life."

"Oh yes. Then he's a friend of Percy Kellynch? But that doesn't tell me what I want to know. WHO is he?"

With a flash of inspiration she said:

"Oh yes! Oh, he's a *nephew* of Lord Wantage. He has no father and mother, I believe. He and his brother Charlie——"

"Ah yes, yes. It comes back to me now—I remember which Hilliers they are. Well, Hillier has asked me to dine with him and go to the Russian Ballet. Rather nice of him. I'm going, and—do you know why I accepted, Madeline?"

"You like the Russian Ballet."

"I was told that Mrs. Kellynch and *you* were to be of the party."

"I'm glad you're going," she answered. "Bertha's so awfully kind——" She stopped suddenly, as if she had made a *gaffe*.

He smiled. "Really? And what has Bertha's kindness to do with it?"

"Oh, nothing. I mean she always takes me out wherever she can; she's so good-natured."

"She strikes me as being a very beautiful and brilliant person," said Rupert coldly. "Very wonderful—very delightful. . . . It appears that Mrs. Hillier has influenza."

"Oh yes," said Madeline quickly—too quickly.

"You knew it? No; you thought that she probably *would* have," said he, laughing, as he struck a match. Then he leant back, smoking, with that slow, subtle smile about nothing in particular that had a peculiar, hypnotic effect upon Madeline.

She adored him more and more every moment. She knew she was never at her best in his company; he made her nervous, shy, and schoolgirlish, and so modest that she seemed to be longing to ooze away, to eliminate herself altogether. Then he said:

"Well, Madeline, it wouldn't be nice if I kept you too long away from your mother—she won't trust me with you again."

She jumped up.

"Have I been too long?"

"Nonsense, child," he said. "But still——" With one look at the clock he rather hurriedly gave her her belongings.

"I'm going to put you into a nice taxi, and send you home. We shall meet at Hillier's dinner, that will be nice, and we shall see the wonderful ballet together."

She murmured that it would be lovely.

"I should like to drive you home," he said rather half-heartedly, as they stood at the door in the rain; "in fact, I should insist upon doing so . . ."

"Oh no!"

. . . "But I have an appointment with a friend I'm expecting to call for me here. Au revoir, then!"

She went away happy, disturbed, anxious and delighted, as she always was when she had seen him. She ran straight to her dressing-table, took off her hat, put something gold in her hair and tried to look Byzantine.

He returned to the little table. He had it cleared, and ordered fresh tea and cakes. Then he took out his watch.

In about twenty minutes, during which he grew rather nervous and impatient, he rose and went to the door again to greet another guest, who had been invited to tea an hour and a half later than Madeline.

She also was a young girl, good-looking, very dark and rather inclined to fullness in face and figure. When I say that she had handsome regular aquiline features, two thick curtains of black hair drawn over her ears, from which depended long ear-rings of imitation coral, it seems almost unnecessary to add (for this type of girl always dresses in the same way) that she wore a flat violet felt hat, the back of which touched her shoulders, a particularly tight dark blue serge coat and skirt, a very low collar, and lisle thread stockings which showed above low shiny shoes with white spats. In her hands she held a pair of new white gloves, unworn.

She bounced in with a good deal of *aplomb*, and, without apologising for her lateness, began to chatter a little louder than most of the people present, and with great confidence.

"No, not China tea, thanks. I prefer Indian. Oh, not cream cakes; I hate them. Can't I have hot tea-cakes? Thanks. I've no idea what the time is. I've been to Mimsie's studio. She would insist on doing a drawing of me, and I'm sitting to her"—she turned her face a little on one side —"like this, you know."

"Is it like you, Miss Chivvey?"

"Oh, good gracious, I hope not! At least I hope I'm not like *it!* I don't want to have a pretty picture, I'm sure. But Mimsie's awfully clever. It's sure to be all right. Do you know her? I must take you to her studio one day."

"Thanks immensely," said Rupert Denison, a little coolly. "But—it may seem odd to you, but I haven't the slightest desire to increase my acquaintance at my age. In fact, do you know, I think I know quite enough people—in every set," he added.

As he poured out some milk, she jumped and gave a little shriek.

"Oh, *don't* do that. I never take milk. What a bad memory you've got! Funny place this, isn't it?" She was looking round. "I don't think I've ever been here before."

"Don't you like the plan of it?" he said, looking round at the walls and ceiling. "It may not be perfect, but really, for London, it isn't bad. It seems to me that anyone can see that it was designed by a gentleman."

"You mean anyone can see it's not designed by an architect?" she asked, with a laugh so loud that he raised a finger.

He then carefully introduced the subject of hats and advised her to go, for millinery, to Selfridge. They discussed it at length, and it was settled by his offering her a hat as a birthday present. She accepted, of course, with a loud laugh.

Rupert, with his mania for educating and improving young people, had begun, about a fortnight ago, trying to polish Miss Chivvey.

But he had his doubts as to its being possible; and he was, all the same, beginning to be a little carried away. She was sometimes (he owned) amusing; and it was unusual for him to be laughed at. How differently Madeline regarded him!

However, he drove Moona home to Camden Hill and promised to meet her and help her to choose a hat.

"But I sha'n't let you interfere too much. What do men know of millinery?" she asked contemptuously.

"I am sure I know what would suit you," he replied. "You see, you're very vivid, and very much alive; you stand out, so you really want, if I may say so, attenuating, subduing, shading."

"Perhaps you would like me to put my head in a bag?"

"No one would regret that more than I should."

"I foresee we're going to quarrel about this hat," she answered. "Now, Mr. Denison, do let me explain to you, I don't want anything *smart*. I don't want to look like *Paris Fashions*."

"No? What do you want to look like?"

"Why, artistic, of course! What a blighter you are!"

Rupert winced at this vague accusation. They were nearly at her house and he put his hand on hers in a way that was rather controlling than caressing.

"Let me have one little pleasure. Let me choose your hat myself," he said. He was terrified at the idea of what she might come out in on artistic grounds. Then she would tell all her friends it was a present from him! She had no sort of reticence.

"Well, I suppose you must have your own way. Do you really know anything about it?" she asked doubtfully.

"Rather. Everything!"

They arrived. She jumped out.

"Well, I'll ring you up and tell you when I can go there and meet you. Good-bye! You *are* a nut!"

CHAPTER V

A HAPPY HOME

THE first six months after his marriage it used to give Nigel a thrill of gratification and vanity to go home to his house, one of the finest in Grosvenor Street, and splendidly kept up. Then he had suddenly grown horribly sick of it, longed for freedom in a garret, and now he associated it with no thrill of pride or pleasure, but with boredom, depression, quarrels and lack of liberty. Liberty! Ah! That was it; that was what he felt more than anything else. He had married for money chiefly to *get* liberty. One was a slave, always in debt—but it was much worse now. The master of the house lost all his vitality, gaiety and air of command the moment he came into the hall.

"Where's Mrs. Hillier?"

"Mrs. Hillier is in the boudoir, sir."

The boudoir was a little pink and blue Louis Seize room on the ground floor, opposite the dining-room. From the window Mary could watch for Nigel. That was what she always did. She hardly ever did anything else. Few women were so independent of such aids to idleness as light literature (how heavy it generally is!), newspapers, needlework or a piano. Few people indeed had such a concentrated interest in one subject. She was sitting in an arm-chair, with folded hands, looking out of the window. It was a point of vantage, whence she could see Nigel arrive more quickly than from anywhere else.

As soon as he caught the first glimpse of her at the window it began to get on his nerves. It was maddening to be waited for. . . .

"You're five minutes late," she said abruptly, as he came in. She always spoke abruptly, even when she wanted to be most amiable. He was determined not to be bad-tempered, and smiled good-naturedly.

"Am I? So sorry." He was very quick and rapid in every word and movement, but soft and suave—never blunt, as she was.

"Where have you been?"

"I went to look at those pictures in Bond Street," he replied, without a moment's hesitation.

He had come straight from seeing Bertha—on the subject of Madeline and Rupert—but he never thought of telling her that.

"Oh! Why didn't you take *me?*"

"I really don't know. I didn't think of it, I suppose. We'll go another day."

He sat down opposite her and began to smoke a cigarette, having permission always. She sat staring at him with clasped hands and eager eyes.

Bertha's description of her as having flat red hair, a receding chin and long ear-rings was impressionistically accurate. It was what one noticed most. Mrs. Hillier was plain, and not at all pleasant-looking, though she had a pretty figure, looked young, and might have been made something of if she had had charm. There was something eager, sharp and yet depressed about her, that might well be irritating.

She got up and came and stood next to Nigel; playing with his tie, a little trick which nearly drove him mad, but he was determined to hide it. When he couldn't bear it any longer he said: "That will do, dear."

She moved away.

"How do you mean 'that will do'?"

"Nothing; only don't fidget."

"You're nervous, Nigel. You are always telling me not to fidget."

"Am I? Sorry. Where are the children?"

"Never mind the children for a minute. They're out with Mademoiselle."

"Seen much of them to-day?"

"They came in to lunch. No, I have *not*, as a matter of fact. Do you expect me to spend my whole time with children of eight and nine?"

He didn't answer, but it was exactly what he really did expect, and would have thought perfectly natural and suitable.

"Some women," continued Mary, "seem to care a great deal more for their children than they do for their husbands. I'm *not* like that—I don't pretend to be."

Nigel already knew this, to his great regret.

"I care more for you than I do for the children," she repeated.

"Yes."

"What do you mean by 'Yes'?"

"I was assenting: that's all. I meant—that you've told me all this before, my dear. Haven't you?"

"Do you object? Do you *mind* my caring more for you than for the children?"

"If I object to anything it's only to your repeating yourself. I mean—we've had all this; haven't we?"

"Nigel, are you trying to quarrel with me for loving you better than the children?"

Nigel turned pale with irritation but controlled himself and stood up and looked out of the window.

"Not in the least. It's most flattering. I only don't want to be told it every time I see you. . . . I mean that of course I should think it perfectly natural if you were fond of the children too."

"I *am* fond of them," she answered, "but they are not everything to me. They don't fill up my whole time and all my thoughts. They won't do instead of you."

"No one suggested that, I think. Have you been for a drive to-day?"

"No—I haven't."

"What a funny woman you are, Mary! You might as well not have a motor for all the use you make of it."

"I had nowhere to go."

He looked at some invitation cards on the mantelpiece. "Oh, my dear, that's absolute nonsense. You mean you don't care to go anywhere. It *is* extraordinary, how you drop people, Mary! When we first came to this house we had a lot of parties and things. Now you never seem to care for them."

"It's quite true," she answered. "We did have parties and things. They made me miserable. I hated them."

"Rather odd; aren't you?"

"I hated them and loathed them," she continued. "For it only meant there were crowds of women who tried to flirt with you."

"That's an *idée fixe* of yours, my dear. Pure fancy, you know."

"Well; all I know is I hated to see you talking to the women who came here. I tell you, quite frankly, *that's* the reason why I've given up accepting invitations and giving them. Of course, if you *insist*, I will. I would do anything you told me."

"Oh, good God, no! Let's cut out the parties, then. Don't have them for *me*! I thought it would be fun for you. . . . What *do* you do all day, Mary, if I may ask? You never seem to have any shopping—or hobbies—or anything that other women have to do."

"I do the housekeeping in the morning," she said; "I see cook and look after everything to make things as *you* like."

"And I'm sure you do it very well indeed. But it doesn't take long; and after that——?"

"I sit in that chair looking out of the window for you."

He bit his lip impatiently, trying not to be irritable.

"It's very nice of you, Mary, I'm sure. But I do wish you wouldn't!"

"Why not? Don't you *like* me to be waiting for you?"

"No—I don't. I should like to think you were enjoying yourself; having a good time."

"Well, I shouldn't do it if you took me out with you always."

"My dear, I'm always delighted to take you with me, but I can't take you everywhere."

"Where can't you take me?"

"Well—to the club!" He smiled, and took up a newspaper.

"I suppose you must go to your club sometimes," she said rather grudgingly. "But tell me, Nigel, would you like us to go in more for society again as we used at first?"

He thought a moment. There were more quarrels when they saw more people—in fact, the fewer people they met the fewer subjects arose for scenes.

"Well," he said, "suppose you give just one party this year. Just to 'keep our circle together,' as they say—then we can stop it again, if you like."

"What sort of party?"

"Any sort. Musical, if you like."

"Oh! that means having horrid singers and players, and performers! I don't like that set, Nigel."

"All right. Let's give a dance. We've got a splendid floor."

"A *dance*? Oh no. I don't dance; and I couldn't bear to see you dancing with anyone."

"This is all very flattering, my dear, but you know you're really rather absurd. Girls wouldn't be fighting to dance with an old married man like me. Altogether,—the way you regard me,—the way you imagine I'm the marked-down prey of every woman you know, —would be too comical if it wasn't so pathetic."

"Oh, really? So you say! You're thirty-five;—you're better-looking than ever."

"Thanks. It's very kind of you to think so." He laughed rather contemptuously. "What a fatuous idiot I should be if I believed you. But—to go back to what we were talking about—it really is in a way rather a pity you're gradually dropping everybody like that. It seems to me that one should either have a cosy, clever, interesting little set of amusing and really intimate *friends*; or else, a large circle of acquaintances; or both. I'm not speaking of parties, for me. No man of course cares about all that sort of rot; it's only for you; women like going out as a rule."

"I didn't care much about the sort of society you introduced me to when we first married. I didn't like any of them much."

"What's the matter with them?" he asked. He knew she had always felt morbidly and bitterly out of it because she mistakenly believed that everybody was interested in the fact that her grandfather had made a fortune in treacle, and that her husband was Lord Wantage's nephew. As a matter of fact, no one who came to the house cared in the slightest degree about either of these circumstances (even if they knew them) but merely wished candidly to enjoy themselves in a large, jolly, hospitable house, owned by a very attractive man with a large number of amusing friends and, apparently, a harmless and good-natured little wife. Mary detested and soon put a stop to intimate or Bohemian friends who sat up all night smoking, talking art or literature, or being musical; and she managed rapidly to reduce their circle to a much smaller one at a much greater distance. She had not a single intimate friend. With women she only exchanged cards. "What's wrong with them all?" Nigel repeated, for he was beginning to lose patience.

"Oh! their manners are all right. If you really want to know what I think of the whole set—I mean that sort of half-clever, half-smart set you were in—the barristers and writers, artists, sporting and gambling men, and women mad on music and the theatre—well, it is that the men are silly and frivolous, and the women horrid and—and *fast*! Some are cold and just as hard as nails, others are positively *wicked!* I admit most of the men have nice manners and the women are not stupid. They all dress well."

Nigel was silent a moment.

"Well, after all, if you don't like them, why should you see them?" he said, good-naturedly enough. He did not feel inclined to defend all his acquaintances. "But may I ask, do you consider that this set, as you call it, lead a *useless* life?"

"Yes; of course I do."

"Oh! Good. That's all I wanted to know."

"I see what you mean quite well," she said, walking up and down the room. "You think *I* lead a useless life—that I'm not accomplished or literary or even domestic, or social. You think I lead an empty life with all my money."

"Well, why shouldn't you, if you like it? But I wish you enjoyed it yourself more, that's the point."

"I can never enjoy myself—if you want to know, Nigel—except when I'm with you; and even then I'm often not happy, because I think you don't care to be with me."

"Oh, Mary! really! How awful you are! What rot all this is! I can't say more than that you can do whatever you like from morning to night, and that I don't wish to interfere with you in any possible way."

"But I should like you to be *with* me more."

He restrained the obvious retort (that she didn't make herself agreeable).

"Well, I *am* with you." He humoured her gently.

"Yes—at this moment."

"Aren't we going to dine together?"

"Yes, we are. But about an hour afterwards I know you'll find some sort of excuse either to go out, or to go into the library and read. Why can't you read while I'm looking at you? Why not?"

"Don't be always looking forward, meeting troubles half way," he said jokingly. "Perhaps I sha'n't read." Then, after a moment's pause: "Excuse my saying so, my dear, but if *you* sometimes read a book, or the papers, or saw more people, you would have more to tell me when we did meet, wouldn't you?"

"It doesn't matter about that. You can tell me what you've been reading or seeing. Who did you see at the picture gallery? Was Mrs. Kellynch there?"

"Look here"—he was looking at the paper —"would you like to go to the opera after dinner? Let's go one of these days soon."

"No; I shouldn't like it at all."

He stared at her in surprise.

"Why not, pray? I thought you enjoyed it the other night?"

"*You* enjoyed it," she replied.

"I thought you seemed rather pleased with yourself when we went out, with all your furs and tiaras and things. You looked very smart," he said pleasantly.

"Well, I tell you I hated it, Nigel."

"And why?"

Mary was at least candid, and she spoke bluntly.

"Because we met Mrs. Kellynch; and you talked to her and seemed pleased to see her."

"Oh, good heavens! I can hardly cut dead all the women I ever knew before we were married."

"Do you think her pretty?" said Mary.

"Yes, of course I do; and so does everyone. She is pretty. It's a well-known fact. But what does it matter? It's of no interest to me."

"Are you sure it isn't? Didn't you tell me you were almost engaged once?"

"Oh, *do* let's drop the prehistoric," he entreated, appearing bored. "Never mind about ancient history now. She's married and seems very happy." (He stopped himself in time from saying like us.) "Kellynch is a very good sort."

"Is he? Do you envy him?"

"Mary, really, don't be absurd. Let me tell you that there's not one man in a hundred who could stand . . ." and he moved a step farther away.

"Could stand what?" She came nearer to him. "My caring for you so much?"

Half-a-minute passed in something near torture, as she played with his tie again, and he controlled himself and spoke with a determinedly kind smile.

"Go along and dress for dinner," he said.

"What shall I wear?"

"Oh! Your pretty yellow teagown," he answered.

She could not go out in that, he was reflecting, and if he suddenly wanted to go for a walk——

"Very well, Nigel. Oh, dear Nigel! I don't mean to be disagreeable."

"I'm sure you don't," he answered, "let's leave it at that, my dear."

"All right," she said smiling, and went away, with a rather coquettish kiss of the hand to him.

He opened the door and shut it after her, with gallant attention. Then he threw up his arms with a despairing gesture.

"My God! What a woman! Why—why was I such a fool? . . . How much longer *can* I bear it?"

The Hilliers' relatives and intimate friends often said cheerfully about them: "Mary is very fond of Nigel, but she rather gets on his nerves."

No one seemed yet to have discovered that there was a large double tragedy in that simple, commonplace sentence.

CHAPTER VI

FUTURISM

IT had long been Nigel's dream, since he had practically given up all hope of calm and peaceful happiness at home, to have, at least, a secret sorrow that everyone knew of and sympathised with. And certain people did feel for him, understanding the great worry of his wife's morbid jealousy. But the general public thought him extremely fortunate to have married a woman—or rather a young girl—whose enormous wealth was only equalled by her extraordinary devotion. Yet from the one person who mattered, the look of tacit sympathy was denied him. How it would have soothed him and made him absolutely happy! And Bertha was the only human being who must never be allowed to know of his domestic troubles. She was extremely proud, and it would have caused her great anger and pain to think that after throwing her over (as he really had, for worldly advantages), he should then want to come back, complain ungratefully of the benefactress he had chosen and philander and amuse himself again. So he had never referred to his unhappy life. His plan was deeper than that. It was to appear merely the amusing friend, until by some chance, he should feel his way to be more secure; to be, in fact, a kind of tame cat, a *camarade*, useful, and intellectually sympathetic, unselfishly devoted—until, perhaps, the time might come when she might find she could not do without him. His calculations happened to be completely wrong, but that, of course, he could not know. Like all collectors, whether of women or of any other works of art or nature, although a connoisseur, he did not quite recognise the exceptional when he met it—his rules of life were too general. And his love for Bertha—what word can one use but the word-of-all-work, love, which means so many variations and shades, and complications of passion, sentiment, vanity and attraction?—his love had greatly increased, was growing stronger: sometimes he wondered whether it was the mere contradictory, defiant obstinacy of the discouraged admirer; and, certainly, there was in his devotion a strong infusion of a longing to score off his tyrannising wife and the fortunate, amiable Percy. Nigel's jealousy of

Percy—and not of Percy only, but in a less degree of most men Bertha knew—was not very far behind his wife's jealousy of him. A morbid propensity that causes great suffering in domestic life is often curiously infectious to the very person for whom it creates most suffering. Nigel sometimes found himself positively imitating Mary in many little ways; watching, and listening and asking indirect questions to find things out: if he had dared he would have made Bertha a violent scene every time her husband came into the house! He tried to hide it and had made Percy like him. But Bertha could see perfectly well the tinge of jealousy for every other friend of hers, and an inclination to crab and run down and sit out, especially, any smart young man. This neither amused nor annoyed her. She did not think about it.

Nigel really felt, besides, that most cruel of all remorse—*selfish* remorse, that he had cheated himself in having thrown over love for money. For his was not, after all, a mere smug, second-rate nature which gold, and what it meant, in however great quantities, could really ever satisfy. Putting aside the fact that his wife irritated him nearly to madness, even if he had been allowed to live alone, and perfectly free,—wealth and its gratifications would never have made him happy. He had mistaken himself in a passing fit of despair and cupidity, aided by the torturing agonies of being deeply in debt all round, and the ghastly fear of a social smash.

He had a longing to feel at ease; he had a love of pleasure, too, of freedom, of idleness; and the sort of talent that consists in brilliantly describing what one could do and what one would like to do: in sketching schemes, verbally—literary, financial, artistic, no matter what—with so much charm, such aplomb that everyone believed in him, and enjoyed to hear his projects, but he had not either the genius that compels its owner to work nor the steadiness, the determination of character that makes a man a successful drudge, who gets there in the end.

Nigel is being rather severely analysed. But let it be understood that with it all, besides having very great charm of look and manner, wit and high spirits, in certain ways he was quite a good fellow: he had no sneers for the more fortunate, no envy, nothing petty: he was warm-hearted, generous even—when it did not cross some desire of his; lavish with money, both on himself and on anyone who aided his pleasure, and quite kind and tender-hearted in that he couldn't bear to see anyone suffer—even Mary, with whom, as a matter of fact, he was very weak.

The saint thinks only of the claims of others: the criminal solely of his own. Between these extremes, there are, obviously, countless shades. Unfortunately, Nigel had this in common with the worst; that when he really wanted anything, everything had to go to the wall: all rights of others, principles and pity were forgotten, everything was thrown over—everyone pushed out of the way. He became unscrupulous. So when he had required money he threw over his first love who,he knew, adored him; now when he found out the mistake and was seriously in love with Bertha, he would have thrown over anything on earth to get her, and admired himself for doing it. He thought himself now noble-spirited and sporting. He would have run away with her at any moment, even if he thought they would have two or three hundred a year to live on, or nothing at all. Not only that, he would have been devoted to her and worshipped her and never reproached her—and been faithful to her too—until he fell in love with someone else, which might, or might not have happened.

Often he wondered why he cared so much more for Bertha now that she was twenty-eight than when she was eighteen. Perhaps she had really increased in charm: certainly she had in magnetism and in knowledge of the world, and she was just as attractive, a sweet little creature whom one wanted to protect and yet whom, in a way, one could lean on and rely on, too. She was so subtle, so strangely wise and sensible—she seemed to know everything while having the naïve, unconscious air of a person who knows next to nothing. And all these gifts she used—for what? She made Percy happy, she was charming and kind, clear-sighted, indulgent (if a little cynical), and always amusing; full of dash and spirit, and yet with the most feminine softness, and above all that invaluable instinct, always, for doing and saying the right thing . . . and (he knew instinctively) a genius for love. . . .

Yes, he thought, she was an extraordinary woman! There was nobody like her: in his opinion she was thrown away on Percy. But *she* did not think so, and he envied, hated the husband, with an absurd bitterness—envied him for several reasons, but chiefly because Nigel had now developed what had been in abeyance at the time of their youthful engagement—that real sensuous discrimination, which has comparatively little to do with taste for beauty, that power of weighing amorous values, given only to the authentic Sybarite.

On the day arranged for the Russian Ballet party, Nigel made an excuse for seeing Bertha to arrange tactics with regard to Rupert and Madeline. She told him she was expecting the Futurist painter, the Italian, Semolini, but she received him first.

"About Rupert, now," said Nigel. "Isn't it odd?—I always think of Rupert with a rapier concealed somewhere about his person. Ruperts and rapiers are inseparably associated in my mind. Well—shall I, after supper, drive back with Rupert and praise up Miss Irwin—or not?"

"Yes, if you think it is a good thing."

"*If* I think it's a good thing! Nothing in the world has such a good effect on a man as the admiration of another man for the girl he admires."

"But don't do too much digging in the ribs—don't overdo it. Rupert, though he doesn't carry a rapier, isn't quite a modern cynical man, and with all his affectations I believe he has a very sweet nature. He'll be good to Madeline—I want her to be happy."

"Well, at any rate, if she likes him she may as well have her fling at him," said Nigel carelessly.

Bertha looked annoyed.

"That isn't the point only—silly! If she liked *you* ever so much and you were free, do you suppose I would take her side—help her?"

"I hope not," said Nigel insinuatingly, suddenly changing his seat to one close to Bertha.

She looked calmly away, as if bored.

He saw it was the wrong tone and stood up, with his back to the mantelpiece, looking at her.

"I like your frock, Bertha."

She looked down at it.

"You have an extraordinary air of not knowing what you have got on. I never saw a woman look so unconscious of her dress. There's a good deal of the art that conceals art about it, I fancy. Your clothes are attractive—in an impressionist way!"

"The only thing I think of about my dresses, is that they should make people admire me—not my dressmaker," said Bertha candidly. "I don't care for much variety, and I leave real smartness to Madeline and the other tall, slim girls. My figure is so wrong! How dare I be short and tiny, and yet not thin, nowadays?"

"You're exquisite—at least in my opinion. I've never been an admirer of the lamp-post as the type of a woman's figure."

She looked bored again. "Oh, please don't! I don't care what you like—so long as you like

Mary, who was very graceful and *chic*, I thought, the other night at the opera."

It was Nigel's turn to look bored.

"Yes. . . . What is this chap like, this Semolini man?"

"He's not like anything. He's a nice little thing."

"Signor Semolini," announced the servant.

A very small, very brown young man came in, clean-shaven, with large bright blue eyes, black hair, and a single eyeglass with a black ribbon.

They greeted him cordially, convinced him that he was welcome, made him feel at home, gave him tea. It was his first visit, but no one was ever shy long with Bertha. He soon began chattering very volubly in a sort of English, which, if not exactly broken, was decidedly cracked.

"I like those things of yours—at the gallery, I mean," said Nigel patronisingly. He was always patronising to all artists, even when he didn't know them, as in this case, to be cranks. "I think they're top-hole; simply *awfully* good, I thought. I didn't quite understand them, though, I admit."

"But you saw ze idea?"

"What idea?"

"Why, the simultaneity of the plastic states of mind in the art? That is our intoxicating object, you know."

"Oh, that! Ah, yes—yes, quite so. I thought it was that." Nigel looked knowing, and shook his head wisely.

Under this treatment the young Italian became very animated.

"You were right! You see, it is ze expansion of coloured forms in space, combined with the co-penetration of plastic masses which forms what we call futurism."

"Oh yes, of course," said Nigel. "It would be. I mean to say—well!—almost anyone would guess that, wouldn't they?"

Semolini turned to Bertha, talking more and more quickly, and gesticulating with a little piece of bread and butter in his right hand. "It is ze entire liberation from the laws of logical perspective that makes movement—the Orphic cubism—if you will allow me to say so!"

"Oh, certainly," smiled Bertha. "*Do* say so!"

"Orphic cubism! I say! Isn't that a bit strong before a lady?" murmured Nigel.

Semolini laughed heartily without understanding a word, and continued to address himself to Bertha, whose eyes looked sympathetic. "It is painting, pure painting—painting new masses with elements borrowed chiefly from the reality of mental vision!" cried the artist.

"Funny! Just what I was going to say!" said Nigel.

Bertha contented herself with encouraging smiles.

The young Italian was due to lecture on his views, and had to leave. At least three appointments were made with him, none of which Nigel had the slightest intention of keeping—to "go into the matter more thoroughly"—then Semolini vanished, charmed with his reception.

"Good heavens! will someone take me away and serve me up on a cold plate?" said Nigel, directly he had gone. "Look here, Bertha, is the chap off his head, a fraud, or serious?"

"Awfully serious. Are you going to see him to look into the matter?"

"I *think* not," said Nigel, "at least I don't want to see his pictures, face to face, until I've insured my life. I must think of my widow and the children."

Here Nigel's young brother, Charlie, arrived. He was a slimmer, younger, but less good-looking edition of Nigel. He had just come down from Oxford, was pleasant, gentle, and appeared to be trying to repress a natural inclination to be a nut. He called on Bertha in the hope of seeing Madeline.

"I say, the Futurist chap has just been here," said Nigel to Charlie.

"Good! What's he like?"

"A little bit of all right. Frightfully fascinating, as girls say," said Nigel.

"He's not so bad," said Bertha mildly.

"Isn't he? I've seen the pictures. But what *is* he like? The sort of chap you'd like to be seen with?" asked the young man.

"Well—not acutely," replied Nigel.

"Very dark, is he? quite black?"

"Yes."

"Good teeth?"

"Yes, several."

"Clean-shaven?"

"Not very."

There was a pause.

"But is he really an Italian?" asked Charlie.

"Shouldn't think so," said Nigel carelessly.

"What then?" asked Bertha, laughing.

"Scotch, probably."

"Very likely, if he's clever. They say all the clever people come from Scotland," Charlie remarked.

"And the cleverer they are, the sooner they come, I suppose," said Bertha. "Fancy the MacFuturist in a kilt!"

"But where does he come from . . . where does he really live?" continued Charlie, who seemed to have a special, suspicious curiosity on the subject.

"Rapallo," said Bertha.

"Where's that?"

"The first turning to the left on the map as you go to Monte Carlo," said Nigel.

"But what *did* he say—was he very odd and peculiar?"

"Oh, he carried on like one o'clock about Futurism," said Bertha.

"I thought every moment would be my next," said Nigel.

"What nonsense you're both talking," said Bertha.

"Yes, and if Charlie thinks he's going to sit me out by asking questions, he's jolly well mistaken," Nigel said. "Look here, old chap, Bertha's going out. I know she wants to get into her glad raiment. I'll drop you."

"Right-o!" said Charlie, jumping up.

They took their leave. Bertha looked amused.

CHAPTER VII

RUSSIAN BALLET

ARRANGEMENTS had been made that Mrs. Nigel Hillier was to have a little dinner at home for her mother (with whom Nigel was not supposed to be on terms); and she and her parent were to go to the St. James's Theatre, for which two stalls had been purchased. Nigel pretended he was dining with an old friend at the club.

Coming in brightly, but, as usual, losing half his personality in the hall, he found Mary at seven o'clock sitting in the little boudoir, in the usual arm-chair, looking out for him, not, apparently, thinking of dressing for dinner.

"Hallo, Mary!" he said. "Hadn't you better get ready for your mother?"

"No," she responded rather coldly and bitingly, "I've put mother off."

He glanced at her with self-control. She looked, he thought, far more bitter than usual.

"That's a pity, because you will be alone—dear. Besides, the stalls will be wasted."

"No, they won't," she said. "You'll stay at home with me, and take me to the St. James's. You can easily put off your man at the club." She looked him full in the eyes.

Colour rose to his face and then faded away.

"I'm sorry, my dear, but that's impossible."

"It isn't impossible—you mean you don't want to do it. . . . Oh, do please—please, Nigel!" She came towards him and played with his tie—the trick of hers that he hated most.

She mistook his silence, which was hesitation as to what plan to adopt, for vacillation, and thought she was going to win. . . .

"Oh, 'oo will, 'oo will!" she exclaimed, with a rather sickly imitation of a spoilt child, with her head on one side. It was a pose that did not suit her in any way.

He drew back; the shiny red hair gave him a feeling of positive nausea. She was attempting to defeat him—she was trying to be coquettish—poor thing! . . . She suspected something; she hadn't put off her mother for nothing. . . . He was going to the Russian Ballet with Bertha—how could he leave Bertha in the lurch? With Madeline and Rupert, too—what harm was there in it? (The fact that he heartily wished there *was* had really nothing to do with the point.)

Husbands and wives usually know when opposition is useless. Mary privately gave it up when she heard Nigel speak firmly and quickly—not angrily.

"I've made the arrangement now, and I can't back out."

"And what about me?" she said, in a shrill voice.

He went out of the room hastily, saying:

"I can't help it now; if you alter your arrangements at the last minute—stop at home and read a book, or take some friend to the St. James's."

He ran upstairs like a hunted hare; he was afraid of being late. He had got his table at the Carlton.

Left alone in the boudoir, a terrible expression came over Mary's face. She said to herself quite loudly:

"He is not going to the club; he'd give it up if he were. It's something about that woman . . ."

A wave of hysteria came over her, also a half-hearted hope of succeeding still by a new kind of scene. . . .

There were two large china pots on the mantelpiece; she threw them, first one, then the other, at the half-open door, smashing them to atoms. Excited at her own violence, she ran upstairs screaming, regardless of appearance:

"You sha'n't go! You sha'n't go! I hate you. I'll kill myself. Oh—oh—oh! Nigel! Nigel!"

At eight to the minute Nigel in the Palm Court received Bertha Kellynch dressed in black, Madeline in white, and Rupert Denison with a little mauve orchid in his buttonhole.

The dinner, subtly ordered, was a complete success, and Madeline Irwin was in a dream of happiness, but Bertha was sorry to see that Nigel, who was usually remarkably moderate in the matter of champagne, and to-night drank even less than usual, had the whole evening a trembling hand. Even at the ballet, where he was more than usually ready to enjoy every shade of the enjoyable, he was not quite free from nervous agitation. He did not drive Rupert home, but let Rupert drop him in Grosvenor Street at twelve-thirty—for a slight supper was inevitable and Rupert had taken them to the Savoy.

Mrs. Hillier was in bed and asleep. The maid said she had been ill and excited. The maid, frightened, had sent for the doctor. His remedy had succeeded in calming her.

The next day Mary seemed subdued, and was amiable. Both ignored the quarrel. Nigel believed it would not occur again. He thought his firmness had won and that she was defeated. He did not understand her.

CHAPTER VIII

PERCY

"I'VE had such a lovely letter from Rupert, Bertha. I'm so excited, I can't read it almost!"

Bertha held out her hand. Madeline was looking agitated.

"He says," said Madeline, looking closely at the letter in her short-sighted way, "that he wishes he could burn me like spice on the altar of a life-long friendship! Fancy!"

"Rather indefinite, isn't it?"

"Oh, but listen!" And Madeline read aloud eagerly: "*Yesterday evening was perfect: but to-day and for several days I shall be unable to see you. Why is a feast day always followed by a fast?*"

"Is it Doncaster to-morrow?" asked Bertha.

"Don't be absurd, that's nothing to do with it. Listen to this. *What a curiously interesting nature you have! Am I not right when I say that I fancy in time, as you develop and grow older, you may look at life eye to eye with me?*"

"Madeline dear, *please* don't mistake that for a proposal. I assure you that it isn't one."

Madeline looked up sharply. "Who said it was? But, anyhow, it shows interest. He must be rather keen—I mean interested—in me. It's all very well to say it means nothing, but for a man nowadays to sit down and write a long letter all about nothing at all, it must have some significance. Look how easily he might have rung up! I know you're afraid of encouraging me too much, and it's very kind of you—but I must confess I *do* think that letters mean a great deal. Think of the trouble he's taken. And there's a great deal about himself in it, too."

"Of course, Madeline, I don't deny that it does show interest, and he probably must be a little in love with someone—perhaps with himself—to write a letter about nothing. As you say, it's unusual nowadays. But you mustn't forget that, though Rupert's young, he belongs to the '95 period. Things were very different then. People thought nothing of writing a long letter; and a telegram about nothing was considered quite advanced and American."

"Oh, bother!" said Madeline, "I hate being told about the period he belongs to. It makes it seem like ancient history. Listen to what he says about you—such lovely things! '*Mrs. Kellynch is a delightful contrast to you, and is all that is charming and brilliant, in a different way. Is she not one of those (alas, too few) who are always followed by the flutes of the pagan world?'"*

"That's really very sweet of him. I say, I wonder what it means exactly?"

"I have no idea. But it just shows, doesn't it?"

With a satisfied smile, Madeline put the letter away. Bertha did not press to see it, but remarked: "I see he didn't sign himself very affectionately. Evidently there's nothing compromising in the letter."

"Why do you say that?"

"Because you put it away. Otherwise you would have shown it to me. Nobody cares to show an uncompromising love-letter—with a lukewarm signature."

"At any rate," said Madeline, gliding over the point and leaving the letter in its cover, "your taking us out last night was a very great help. I feel I've made progress; he thinks more of me."

"Yes, I thought it would be a good thing to do. Now you'd better not answer the letter, and please don't show any anxiety if you don't see him for a little while, either."

"I sha'n't be a bit anxious, Bertha, especially if it's only racing, or something of that sort.

Or, in fact, anything, unless I get afraid he's seeing Miss Chivvey. Do you ever think that Rupert still takes an interest in Miss Chivvey?"

"A little, but I don't think it matters. I think she's needed as a contrast to you. She surprises and shocks him, and that amuses him, but she isn't his real taste. I don't think Miss Chivvey's dangerous, seriously. She uses cheap scent."

"Oh!" cried Madeline, delighted. "There's nothing so awful as cheap scent!"

"Except expensive scent, because it's stronger," said Bertha.

Madeline looked at her admiringly.

"How extraordinary you are, Bertha! It's wonderfully sweet of you to take such an interest in my wretched little romance. You might have so many of your own, if you cared to."

"Ah, but I don't care to. I'm rather exacting in a way, but I don't want variety. I've no desire for an audience. I don't want a little of everybody. All I want is the whole of one person."

"Is that all! Well, you've got it," replied Madeline.

"I hope so," she answered, rather seriously. "I'm not altogether satisfied. I can't settle down to the idea of a dull, humdrum sort of life—and of Percy's being fond of me casually."

"Oh, good gracious, I'm sure he isn't casual! What a strange idea of yours!"

"I hope I'm wrong. I believe I want something that's very nearly impossible. I've always had a sort of ideal or dream of making an ordinary average married life into a romance."

"Well, and can't it be?"

"I don't really see why it shouldn't. But there's no doubt there are immense difficulties in the way. It seems to be necessary, first of all, for there to be not only one exceptional temperament, but two. And that's a good deal to expect. Of course, the obvious danger is the probability of people getting tired of anything they've got. I'm afraid that's human nature. The toys the children see in the shop-window always seem much less wonderful when they're home in the nursery. As a brother of mine used to say a little vulgarly, 'You don't run after an omnibus when once you've caught it'."

"Perhaps not."

"As soon as you belong to a person, obviously, Madeline, they don't value you *quite* in the same kind of way. The glamour seems to go."

"But you don't want necessarily always to be *run after*, surely? You want to be treasured and valued—all that sort of thing."

"Yes, I know! But my ideal would be that there should be just as much excitement and romance and *fun* after marriage as before—if it were possible."

"Oh, good heavens, Bertha! then, if one were to go by that horrible theory of your brother's, one ought never to marry the person one loves, if one wants to keep them."

"No, in theory, one ought not. But then, where are you if he goes and marries someone else? After all, you'd rather he got tired of *you* than of the other person! Wouldn't you prefer he should make *your* life miserable than any other woman's? Besides, one must take a risk. It's worth it."

"I should think it is, indeed!" cried Madeline. "Why, I would marry Rupert if I thought I should never see him again after a month or two—if I knew for a fact he would get tired of me!"

"Of course you would, and quite right too. But remember people are not all alike. There are any number of men who are absolutely incapable of being really in love with anyone who belongs to them. They simply can't help it. It's the instinct of the chase. And it's mere waste of time and energy to attempt to change them."

"Are you speaking of men or husbands?"

"Either, really. But don't let's forget that there are a great many others, on the other hand, who care for nothing and no one who isn't their own. Collectors, rather than hunters. Surely you've noticed that, Madeline? It's a passion for property. The kind of man who thinks *his* house, *his* pictures, *his* cook, even his mother, everything connected with him must be better than the possessions of anyone else. Well, this kind of man is quite capable of remaining very devoted to his own wife, and in love with her, if she's only decently nice to him; and even if she's not. I mean the sort of man one sometimes sees at a party, pointing out some utterly insignificant person there, and declaring that Gladys or Jane, or whoever it is, takes the shine out of everyone else, and that there's no one else in the room to touch her. His wife, of course. I don't mean out of devotion—that's another, finer temperament—but simply and solely because she belongs to him."

"Well, Bertha, I don't care what his reason is, I *like* that man!"

"Oh, rather! So do I. And very often he's not a bit appreciated; though he would be by us. Perhaps the most usual case of all is for the husband, if he's married for love, to remain in love for the first two or three years, and for the love then to turn gradually into a warm friendship, or even a deep affection, which may go on growing deeper—it's only the romance and the glamour and sparkle that seems to go—the excitement. And that's such a pity. I can't help thinking in many cases it really needn't be. More often than not, I believe, it's the woman's mistake. Just at first, she's liable to take too much advantage of the new sort of power she feels."

"Do you mean, Bertha, that the woman generally doesn't take enough trouble with the house to make it pleasant for him at home—and all that?"

"I *didn't* mean that, though it might be so. But sometimes it's just the other way. More often than not she takes a great deal too much trouble about the home, and bothers him about it. There's far too much domesticity. It's like playing at houses at first, but soon it grows tedious. At any rate the whole thing is worth studying very deeply. I can tell you I haven't given it up yet."

"You? Oh, Bertha, I can't think what fault you have to find. You, as you say, certainly are exacting."

"I blame myself, solely. I feel that, somehow or other, I've allowed things to get too prosaic. Percy takes everything for granted: everything goes on wheels. Of course, if I were satisfied to settle down at twenty-eight with complete contentment at the prospect of a humdrum existence, it would be all right; but I'm not. In another few years Percy will be getting on very well as a barrister, taking himself seriously, and regarding me just as part of the furniture at home. You know he always calls me a canary; that shows his point of view. Well, then, he might get a little interested in a wilder kind of bird, and I shouldn't like it!"

"What would your idea be, then? Would you flirt to make him jealous?"

"No, I certainly shouldn't. That's frightfully obvious and common. If I ever did flirt, it wouldn't be for such a silly reason as that. It would be for my own amusement and for nothing else, but I don't think I ever shall. I think it's a fatal mistake for a woman to lower herself in any way in the other person's eyes. Her lasting hold and best one, is that he must think her perfection; it's the safest link with a really nice man. Anyone can be worse than you are, but it's not easy when you take the line that none can be *better!* because no one else is going to try! But if, after all, he still gets tired of her, as they sometimes do, well—it's very hard—but I am afraid she must manage badly."

"I never should have dreamed you thought of all these things, Bertha. You seem so serene and happy."

"I am. It's the one subject I ever worry about. I'm always prepared for the worst."

"And I'm quite sure you've no cause to be. Why not wait till trouble comes?" suggested Madeline.

"Why, then it would be too late. No, I want to ward it off long before there's any danger."

"I think it's very unlike you—almost morbid—bothering about possibilities that will never happen."

"I daresay it is, in a way. But, you know, I fancy I've second sight sometimes. What I feel with us is that things are too smooth, too calm, a little dull. Something ought to happen."

"You're looking so pretty, too," said Madeline rather irrelevantly.

"I'm glad to hear it; but I only want one person to think so."

"But it's obvious that he does; he's very proud of you."

"I sometimes think he's too much accustomed to me. He takes me as a matter of course."

"If that is so, I daresay you'll be able to alter matters," said Madeline, getting up to go.

"Yes, I daresay I shall; it only needs a little readjusting," Bertha said.

They shook hands in cordial fashion. They did not belong to the gushing school, and, notwithstanding their really deep mutual affection, neither would ever have dreamed of kissing the other.

As soon as Madeline had gone Bertha went and looked steadily and seriously in the glass, for some considerable time. She thought on the whole that it was true that she was looking pretty: on this subject she was perfectly calm, cool and unbiassed, as if judging the appearance of a stranger. For, though she naturally liked to be admired, as all women do, she was entirely without that fluffy sort of vanity, that weak conceit, so indulgent to itself, that makes nearly all pretty women incapable of perceiving when they are beginning to go off, or unwilling to own it to themselves.

The one person for whose admiration and interest she cared for more and more, her Percy, she fancied was growing rather cooler. This crumpled rose-leaf distressed her extremely.

At this moment he arrived home. She heard his voice and his step, and waited for him to come up, with an increasing vividness of colour and expression, with a look of excited animation, that in so sophisticated a woman was certainly, after ten years, a remarkable tribute to a husband.

Percy, who was never very quick, was this evening much longer coming upstairs than usual. He was looking at the letters in the hall. With his long, legal-looking, handsome face, his even features, his fine figure and his expression of mild self-control, and the large, high brow, he had a certain look of importance. He appeared to have more personality then he really had. His manner was impressive, even when one knew—as Bertha certainly did—that he was the mildest, the most amiable and good-natured of serious barristers.

With one of those impulses that are almost impossible to account for, Percy took one of the letters up before the others. It was directed in type. He half opened it, then put it in his pocket. He felt anxious to read it; for some quite inexplicable reason he felt there was something about it momentous, and of interest. It was not a circular, or a bill. It made him feel uncomfortable. After waiting a moment he opened it and read part of it. Then he replaced it in his pocket, and ran up to his room, taking the other unopened letters with him.

"Percy!" called Bertha, as he passed the drawing-room.

"I shall be down in a few minutes," he called out.

He went upstairs and shut himself into his room.

She also felt unaccountably uncomfortable and anxious, as if something had happened, or was going to happen. Why was Percy so long?

When he came down at last she gave him his tea and a cigarette and noticed, or perhaps imagined, that he looked different from usual. He was pale. Yes, he was distinctly a little pale. Poor Percy!

Instead of telling him he was not looking very well, and asking him what was the matter, complaining that he had not taken any notice of her, or behaving otherwise idiotically, after the usual fashion of affectionate wives, she remained silent, and waited till he seemed more as usual.

Then he said: "Has anyone been here to-day?"

"No one but Madeline. She's only just gone."

"Oh yes—been out at all?"

"I went out this morning for a little while."

He seemed absent.

"You enjoyed yourself last night, didn't you?" he asked.

"Oh yes, it was rather fun. Yet, somehow, the Russian Ballet never leaves me in good spirits for the next day. It doesn't really leave a pleasant impression somehow—an agreeable flavour."

"Doesn't it—why?"

"One wants to see it, one is interested, from curiosity, and then, afterwards, there's a sort of Dead Sea-fruitish, sour-grapes, autumn-leaves, sort of feeling! It's too remote from real life and yet it hasn't an uplifting effect. At any rate it always depresses me."

He gave her a rather searching look, and then said:

"Did Hillier like it?"

"I think he enjoys everything. He's always so cheery."

"And to-night we're dining at home?"

"Oh yes, I hope so. We'll have a quiet evening."

After a moment Percy said, in a slightly constrained way:

"I think I shall have to go out for half-an-hour. I want to see a man at the club."

"Oh, must you? But it's raining so much. Why don't you ring him up and ask him to come here?"

She was anxious not to betray a womanish fear that he might be getting influenza, as she knew that nothing would annoy him so much as bothering about him.

"No; I must go out."

She dropped the subject. He took up a new book she had been reading and talked about it somewhat pompously and at great length. The whole time it struck her he was not like himself. Something was wrong. He was either worried, or going to be ill. He had either a temper or a temperature. But she did not refer to it. Dinner was sometimes a good cure for such indispositions.

He continued to make conversation in a slightly formal way until he went out. After he had gone she observed to herself that his manner had varied from polite absent-mindedness to slight irritability. He had gone out without telling her anything about his plans. He had not even kissed her.

CHAPTER IX

AN ANONYMOUS LETTER

MRS. HILLIER habitually had breakfast in her own room, for no particular reason, but because Nigel encouraged her in this luxurious manner of beginning the day. He said a woman ought not to have to come down until the day had been a little warmed, and got ready for her; that she should have time to choose her clothes to harmonise with her moods—time, after a look at the weather, and hearing the news of the day, to settle on what the moods should be. For a man, on the contrary, he thought it ridiculous and weakly idle—indolent in a way not suited to a man. A man, according to Nigel, ought no more to have his breakfast in bed than to come down with a bow of blue ribbon in his hair, or to go and lie down before dressing for a dinner-party.

However, one morning it darted suddenly into Mary's head that Nigel, on going downstairs to breakfast, while she did not, had nearly an hour to himself. What a horrible idea! What injustice to her! And it occurred to her that for years she had never seen Nigel open his letters. She had, indeed, not the slightest idea what his manner at breakfast was like. Was this fair? He always managed to get out of any invitation to the country which included them both.

As soon as she had thought of this, she rang for her maid, and dressed in the wildest hurry, as though she had to catch a train: leaving her tray on the little table untouched, the maid running after her to fasten hooks, and buttons, to stick in pins, and tie ribbons, as though they were playing a game.

Mary won. She was flying out of the room when the maid ran after her, saying:

"Madame, your tortoiseshell comb is falling out of your hair; won't you let me finish dressing it?"

"Don't worry, Searle. What *does* it matter?"

She flew downstairs.

Nigel looked up with that intense surprise that no one can succeed in disguising as the acutest pleasure.

"Well, by Jove," he said, in his quick way, which was so cool and casual that it almost had the effect of a drawl. He looked at her closely, and said reassuringly:

"After all, it may not be true; and if it is, it may be for the best."

"What may not be true, Nigel. What do you mean?"

"Why, this sudden bad news."

"What news? There is no news."

"Isn't there? By Jove, this is splendid! Just come down to have breakfast with me, then! Capital. What will you have, dear?"

He rang the bell.

"Are you sorry to see me?" she asked, darting looks at the envelopes by his plate, looks that were almost sharp enough to open them.

"Sorry to see you? Don't be absurd! Your comb's falling into the sugar basin, and I shouldn't think it would improve the taste of the coffee. Look out! Help! Saved! Mary dear, why don't you do your hair?"

"I was afraid you might go out before I came down."

"Why, I'm not going out for ages, yet."

He gave her his letters in their envelopes, with a half-smile.

"I don't want to see them," she said. "Why do you pass me the letters, as though you thought I came down for that?"

Nigel pretended not to hear. He opened the newspaper.

"I thought," she went on, "it seemed rather a shame that I should always have breakfast upstairs, and leave you alone, without anyone to keep you company."

"Awfully kind of you, but, really, I don't mind a bit."

He gave a quick look round the room. He had again that curious, bitter sensation of being trapped. Was he now not even going to have this pleasant morning hour to himself?

Probably there was not a prettier room in London than this one. It had the pale pink and green, blue and mauve colouring of spring flowers; the curved shapes of the dainty artificial creatures who lived for fine and trivial pleasure only; the best Louis Quinze decoration. And to-day it was a lovely day; and the warm west wind blew in the breath of the pink and blue hyacinths in the window-boxes. There was that pleasant gay buzzing sound of London in June outside in Grosvenor Street: the growing hum of the season, that made one feel right in it, even if one wasn't. Everything was peacefully happy, harsh and hard things seemed unreal; the world seemed made for birds and butterflies, light sentiment, colour, perfume and gay music. In this London life seemed like a Watteau picture.

Nigel saw that he had never yet realised why he was so fond of this room, where he always had breakfast. It was because there he was free, and alone.

Now he was determined that there should be no quarrelling to-day. It is only fair to Nigel to say that he was always quite determined to keep away the quarrels; and fought against them. Placed as they were, with such infinitely more possibilities of happiness than nine *ménages* out of ten—though leaving out unfortunately one, and that the most important part—love—it was terrible that they should quarrel. He was so easy-going, so ready to ignore her faults, to make the best of things as they were. And she liked to quarrel, merely because it made her, for the time, of importance to him. In fact, being madly in love with him, and both wildly and stupidly jealous, to get up a quarrel was almost the only satisfaction she ever had, the only effect she ever produced now.

Since the other evening, when she had behaved with entire want of self-control, or, perhaps, rather with a kind of instinctive premeditated hysteria, she appeared to recognise that manner had not been a real success. She had tried, at all costs, to prevent him going to the theatre, and had failed.

The next day they ignored the trouble; and for some time afterwards she seemed pleasanter, while he was kind and attentive, believing she had really forgotten her grievance.

On the contrary, it was more firmly fixed in her mind than before. She was absolutely determined that, on no excuse whatever, should he continue to see Bertha Kellynch.

She had found out that the host of the evening at the ballet had been Rupert Denison, and that Madeline Irwin, Bertha and Nigel were the guests. For more than a week Mary had entirely given up the quarrelsome and nagging mood, so that Nigel believed she no longer had this absurd fancy about Bertha. As a matter of fact, for the first time, she had really been dissembling, had spent a good deal of time and money in finding out how both Bertha and Nigel spent their time. What little she had found out had given her an entirely false impression, and that had resulted in a very desperate determination. She meant to carry it out this morning. But she wanted to talk a little more to Nigel first.

"Nigel dear, you know what you said the other evening about giving parties?"

"Yes."

"I've been thinking, perhaps, dear, you're right. I find I've dropped nearly all your old friends. I think we'd better give one big party—a reception, I think. Our drawing-room has never been seen yet."

Nigel looked up, really pleased to see her taking a more normal sort of interest in her existence.

"By Jove! I am glad. That's capital! Yes, of course. To start with we'll give an At Home, as they call 'em."

"Do you think there ought to be any sort of entertainment, Nigel?"

"Well, just as you like. You said you didn't want music. . . . How would it be to have a band to play the whole evening?"

"Yes, that would do very well. Oh, and, Nigel! I find I've been so careless and forgotten all the addresses and lost the cards of people that we used to know. I shall want someone to help me."

"Yes, I suppose Mademoiselle won't do."

"Oh no, she's no use. I shall engage a type-writer to go through the list with me and send out cards."

"Right-o! good idea."

He was quite surprised and satisfied, and thought to himself how wise it was of him the other day to ignore the absurd fit of excitement when she had smashed the vases. Certainly she had been better ever since.

"You'd like me to help you with the list, wouldn't you, dear?" he said presently.

She gave him a sharp look.

"I suppose we'd better ask everybody we know to this sort of thing," she said.

"Your mother and I are not on the best of terms, I'm afraid. But you must be sure to ask her, and we'll make it up."

Nigel thought to himself that really would be only fair, considering that he had practically and ingeniously invented the quarrel on purpose; in order that he could have an excuse to go out when Mary's mother came to see her. But, really, Nigel liked her personally and knew that she liked him, and that she was not without sympathy for anyone who had to live with her daughter.

"I suppose you'll want me to ask the Kellynches?" asked Mary, in a rather low voice.

"It would look natural if you did. But, really, I have seen so little of them for the last few years that you can please yourself about it."

"You've accepted several invitations from them," said Mary, in rather a cutting tone. "Perhaps it would be as well to return them."

"I don't think I've ever dined there," said Nigel casually.

"Didn't you meet them that night at the Russian Ballet? Don't deny it! I know you all went to supper at the Savoy."

"Who's denying it! You know that Denison asked me to supper at the Savoy, and that Madeline Irwin was there, and Mrs. Kellynch."

"Quite a nice little *partie carrée*," said Mary, unable to keep up her plan of self-control, and speaking in a trembling voice.

"Now, Mary, don't be absurd! You know it's hardly usual for a bachelor like Rupert to ask three women or three men to supper!"

"I suppose he drove Miss Irwin home?" said Mary, commanding herself as well as she could.

"No, he didn't. Why should he? Mrs. Kellynch who is Madeline's intimate friend, naturally drove Miss Irwin home in her caro And Rupert, who lives near here, dropped me. It was some little time ago, by the way, but I remember it quite well. Nice feller Rupert—we ought to ask him, too."

"All right, dear."

They parted amiably.

An hour later Mary was going through her lists of cards and addresses with the typewriter when she suddenly said:

"Oh, Miss Wilson, I'm writing a sort of story. And it's to be told in a series of letters."

"Oh yes."

"Will you please take this down. This is the address: Percy Kellynch, Esq., 100 Sloane Street. It begins like this: 'Dear Mr. Kellynch——' "...

CHAPTER X

MASTER CLIFFORD KELLYNCH

LADY KELLYNCH was in the room she usually chose for sitting in for any length of time, when her son, Clifford (twelve years old), was at home for the holidays.

A widow, handsome and excessively dignified, as I have mentioned, with her prim notions, she was essentially like the old-fashioned idea of an old maid. As her fine house was very perfectly and meticulously furnished, she treated the presence of Clifford as an outrage in any room but this particularly practical and saddle-bag old apartment, where there was still a corner with a little low chair in it, and boxes full of toys and other things, which were not only far outgrown by Clifford, but which were absolutely never seen nowadays at all, and would be considered far behindhand as amusements for a child of four.

This extra, additional child, born eighteen years after his brother, and just before the death of his father, was still looked upon by Lady Kellynch as a curious mixture of an unexpected blessing, an unnecessary nuisance, and a pleasant surprise. She was always delighted to see him when he first came home from school, but he was very soon allowed to go and stay with Bertha and Percy. Bertha adored him and delighted in him in reality; Lady Kellynch worshipped him in theory, but though she hardly knew it herself, his presence absolutely interfered with all her plans about nothing, spoilt her little arrangements for order, and jarred on the clockwork regularity of her life, especially in her moments of sentiment.

He was a very good-looking boy, with smooth black hair and regular features like his brother, Percy. Perhaps because he was, according to his mother's view, very much advanced for his age, he regarded her rather as a backward child, to whom it would be highly desirable, but unfortunately practically impossible, to explain life as it is now lived.

Lady Kellynch was doing a peculiar little piece of bead embroidery. She did it every day for ten minutes after lunch with a look at Clifford every now and then, occasionally counting her beads, as if she was not altogether quite sure whether or not he ate them when she wasn't looking. This was the moment that she always chose to have conversation with him, so as to learn to know his character. A couple of suitable books, "The Jungle Book," and "Eric, or Little by Little," were placed on a low table by Clifford's side; but, as a matter of fact, he was reading *The English Review*.

"Clifford darling!"

He put the magazine down, shoving a newspaper over it.

"Well, mother?"

"Tell me something about your life at school, darling."

He glanced at the ceiling, then looked down for inspiration.

"How do you mean?"

"Well, haven't you any nice little friends at school, Clifford—any favourites?"

He smiled.

"Oh, good Lord, mother, of course I haven't! People don't have little friends. I don't know what you mean."

She looked rather pained.

"No friends! Oh, dear, dear, dear! But are there no nice boys that you like?"

"No. Most of them are awful rotters."

She put down her beads.

"Clifford! I'm shocked to hear this. Rotters! I suppose that's one of your school expressions

—you mean no nice boys? Poor little fellow! I shall make a note of that."

He looked up, rather frightened.

"What on earth for?"

"Why, I shall certainly speak to your master about it. Oh! to think that you haven't got a single friend in the school! *All* bad boys! There must be something wrong somewhere!"

"Oh, mummy, for goodness sake don't speak to anybody about it. If you say a word, I tell you, I sha'n't go back to school. I never heard of such a thing! I didn't say they were all bad boys—rot! No. Some of them aren't so bad."

"Well, tell me about one—if it's only one, Clifford."

He thought a moment.

"I'm afraid you'll go writing to the master, as you call it, and get me expelled for telling tales, or something."

"Oh, my darling, of course I won't! Poor boy! tell me about this one."

"There's one chap who's fairly decent, a chap called Pickering."

"To think," she murmured to herself, stroking her transformation, and shaking her head, "to think there should be only one boy fairly decent in all that enormous school!"

"Oh, well! *he's* simply *frightfully* decent, as a matter of fact. Pickering fairly takes it. He's top-hole. There's nothing he can't do."

"What does he do, darling?"

"Oh, I can't exactly explain. He's a bit of all right. It's frightfully smart to be seen with him."

Lady Kellynch looked surprised at this remark.

"Clifford—really! I'd no idea you had these social views. Of course you're quite right, dear. I've always been in favour of your being friends with little gentlemen. But I shouldn't like you to be at all—what is called a snob. So long as he *is* a little gentleman, of course, that's everything."

Clifford laughed.

"I never said Pickering was a gentleman! big or little! You don't understand, mother. I mean it's smart to be seen with him because—oh! I can't explain. He's all right."

His mother thought for a little while, then, having heard that it is right to encourage school friendships at home, so as to know under what influence your boy got, she said:

"Would you like, dear, to have this young Master Pickering to tea here one day?"

He looked up, and round the room.

"Oh no, mother; I shouldn't care for him to come here."

"Why not, dear?"

"Oh, I can't explain exactly; it isn't the sort of place for him."

Lady Kellynch was positively frightened to ask why, for fear her boy should show contempt for his own home, so she didn't go into the matter, but remarked:

"I should think a beautiful house in Onslow Square, with a garden like this, was just the thing for a boy to like."

He shook his head with a humorous expression of contempt.

"Pickering wouldn't go into a *Square* garden, mother!"

She waited a moment, wondering what shaped garden was suited to him, what form of pleasaunce was worthy of the presence of this exceptional boy, and then said, trying to ascertain the point of view:

"Would you take him to see Percy?"

He brightened up directly.

"Percy! Oh yes, rather. I'd like him to see Bertha. I shall ask her to let me take him one day."

Lady Kellynch felt vaguely pained, and envious and jealous, but on reflection realised to herself that probably the wonderful Pickering would be a very great nuisance, and make a noise, and create general untidiness and confusion, in which Bertha was quite capable of taking part; so she said:

"Do so, if you like, dear. You're going to see Bertha soon, aren't you?"

"Yes. I'm going to see her to-day." He quickly put *The English Review* under the cushion, sitting on it as he saw his mother look up from her work.

"Bertha's all right; she's pretty too."

"She's very good and kind to you, I must say," said Lady Kellynch. "As they have asked you so often, I think I should like you to pay her a nice little attention to-day, dear. Take her a pretty basket of flowers."

Clifford's handsome dark face became overclouded with boredom.

"Oh, good Lord, mother! can't you telephone to a florist and have it sent to her, if she's *got* to have vegetables?"

"But surely, dear, it would be nicer for you to take it."

"Oh, mother, it would be awful rot, carting about floral tribs in a taxi all over London."

"Floral tribs? What are floral tribs? Oh, tributes! I see! In a taxi! No. I never dreamt of your doing such a thing. Ridiculous extravagance! Go from Kensington to Sloane Street in a taxi!"

"How did you suppose I'd take it, then?"

"I supposed you'd walk," said Lady Kellynch, in a frightened voice.

"Walk! Great Scott! Walk with a basket of flowers! What next! I didn't know you were bringing me up as a messenger-boy. No, mother, I'm too old to be a boy scout, or anything of that sort. What have you got Warden for? Why don't you send the footman? But far the most sensible way is to ring up the place itself, and give the order."

"No, dear," said Lady Kellynch, rather crushed. She had pictured his entrance with some beautiful flowers to please his sister-in-law. "Never mind; it doesn't matter."

"Mind you," said the spoilt boy, standing up, and looking at himself in the glass. "Mind you I should be awfully glad to give Bertha anything she likes. I don't mind. I'll tell you what I'll do. I'll call in at that place in Bond Street, and get her some chocolates."

"Charbonnel and Walker's, I suppose you mean," said his mother.

He smiled.

"They'll do. Pickering says his brother, who's an artist, is going to do a historical picture for next year's Academy on the subject of 'The First Meeting between Charbonnel and Walker.'"

She looked bewildered.

"Just as you like, my dear. Take her some bonbons if you prefer it. Wait! One moment, Clifford. Bertha hates sweets. She never touches them."

"It doesn't matter," he answered. "I do."

CHAPTER XI

A DISCOVERY

"COME in, old boy!"

Bertha was lying on the sofa reading a large book. She didn't put down either her little feet or the book when her young brother-in-law came in.

He also had a book in his pocket, which he took out. Then he produced a box in silver paper.

"For you," he remarked, and then immediately cut the blue ribbon with a penknife and proceeded to begin the demolition of the chocolates.

"A present for me?" said Bertha.

"Yes," he said, taking a second one rather quickly and glancing at the second row.

"I'm so glad you've got me the kind you like. I hope you've got those with the burnt almonds that you're so particularly fond of?"

"Oh yes, rather!"

"Thanks. That was nice and thoughtful of you; I know they're your favourite sort."

"Yes, they are."

"And what I always think is so nice about you, Clifford," Bertha went on, "is that you're so truly thoughtful. I mean, you never forget your own tastes. You really take trouble to get yourself any little thing you like. You put yourself out."

"Oh—I——"

"Oh no, I'm not flattering you; I really mean it. You're such a nice thoughtful boy. I've seen you take a lot of trouble, rather than deprive yourself of anything you cared for."

"Oh, Bertha!"

"Are you going to stay long to-day?"

"Yes, I am," said Clifford, taking up the book he had brought with him. "As long as I can."

"Oh."

"How long can I?"

"Till dinner, or till anyone turns up that I want to talk to."

"Right-o! But you can send me into another room. I needn't go home, need I?"

She laughed.

"Oh, you silly boy! Of course not."

"I say, have you seen my report?" he asked gravely.

"Some of it. Your mother read out little bits."

"Which little bits?" he asked rather anxiously.

"Oh, the worst of course!" said Bertha. "The purple patches! You're a credit to the family, I don't think!"

"She asked me who was my nicest little friend at school," said Clifford.

"And what did you say?"

"I told her about Pickering. I say, Bertha, . . . can I bring Pickering here?"

"Of course you can."

"May I give him a regular sort of invitation from you, then?"

"Yes, rather. Tell him that I and Percy ask him to come and live here from to-morrow morning for the rest of his natural life. Or, if that doesn't seem cordial enough, we'll adopt him as our only son."

"Oh no! I think that's too much."

"Is it? Well, make it from to-morrow afternoon. Or perhaps we'd better not be effusive; it wouldn't look well. So, instead of that, I'll invite him to go to the Zoological Gardens on Sunday fortnight for an hour, and you and he can have buns and tea at your own expense there. That's not too hospitable and gushing, is it?"

He laughed.

"You do look smart, Bertha!" he remarked. "Your shoes are always so frightfully right. I say, can't you tell mother to wear the same sort of shoes? And tell her to look narrower, and not have such high collars."

"My dear boy, your mother dresses beautifully," said Bertha. "What do you want her to look like?"

"I should like her to look like some of those little cards on cigarette boxes, or like a picture post-card, if you want to know," he admitted candidly.

"That's absurd, Cliff."

"But, Bertha, some of the fellows' mothers do."

"Remember your mother is *Percy's* mother, too."

"Pickering's mother doesn't look much older than you," he replied.

"Oh—what a horrid woman!"

He smiled. "Why do you call her a horrid woman? For not looking older than you?"

"Oh! tell her to mind her own business, and not go interfering with me. I shall look whatever age I choose without consulting her!" Bertha pretended to pout and be offended, and went on reading for a little while.

He took another chocolate and turned a page. She did not ask to see the book.

"That's what I call so jolly about you," presently said Clifford. "When I come to see you, you don't keep asking me questions, or giving me things, or advice, or anything. You do what you like, and I do what I like—I mean to say, we both do just what we like."

"Yes; that's the way to be pleasant companions," said Bertha. "I go your way, and you go mine."

"How's Percy?" the boy asked presently.

"Percy's the same as usual. Only I fancy he seems a little depressed."

Presently Clifford looked up and said:

"Anyway, you'll think it over, Bertha; and see what you decide to do about asking Pickering?"

"Rather!" said Bertha, turning a page absently. "He's rather a wonderful chap, then?"

"Isn't he!"

"What sort?"

"What *sort*?" cried Clifford, dropping his book. "Why, Bertha, I was *with* him, *actually with him*, when he went into the country post office and asked the woman if she would let him have small change for ten shillings, and he found he hadn't the half-sovereign then, but would pay her when he didn't see her again! And then he said if she wouldn't do that, he'd like to buy some stamps, and asked if she'd show him some to choose from. And then he said—I saw him do it—'I'll take those two in the middle—I like the colour.' When she said they were fivepence he said that was too expensive, and he couldn't run to it. And then he wanted to buy some sweets—they sell everything at those country shops—and she wrapped some up for him, and then he said he hadn't got a penny, and would she put it down to Lord Arthur's account—that's an uncle of his who didn't know anything about it, and hadn't got any account. And when she refused, fancy, Bertha! he asked if she'd take stamps, as she seemed fond of them, and when she said she would, he stamped twice on the floor and ran out of the shop, and I ran after him. She *was* angry!"

"He seems a useful boy."

"Rather! His people are frightfully rich, you know," went on Clifford. "When they tease him about it at school, he says he's never allowed to use the same motor twice, and that they're made of solid gold! He chaffs everybody."

Clifford murmured on rather disjointedly, and Bertha read without listening much, occasionally making some remark, when the telephone rang.

Bertha had an extension on the little table next to her sofa.

"Shall I go?" asked Clifford.

"No. Just to the other end of the room."

He obeyed, and fell into the depths of a fat arm-chair.

"That you, Nigel? How is it all going on? Madeline hasn't heard from him lately—not for ages."

"Quite so," answered Nigel's voice. "I've found out something I want you to know. It isn't really serious—at least I'm pretty sure I can put it right, but I'd like to see you about it; it wouldn't take you a moment."

"But is it a thing that may make any difference?" she asked rather anxiously.

"No. Not if it's taken in time," he answered.

"Oh, can't you 'phone about it, Nigel?"

"Not very well, my dear. It really wouldn't take you a minute to hear about it *viva voce.*"

"But you can't keep on calling every day!" cried Bertha, exasperated.

"Quite so. Couldn't you go in for a few minutes to-morrow morning at the Grosvenor Gallery in Bond Street? Say at about eleven or twelve? I won't keep you five minutes, I promise, and you can tell me if you approve of my plan."

"Very well, I'll do that. Quarter-past eleven," added Bertha.

"Only one thing, Bertha, don't tell anyone—not a soul."

"Why not?"

"I'll explain when I see you. But you mustn't mention it. It's nothing—two seconds."

"Oh, all right! But why so many mysteries? You might just as well tell me now on the telephone."

"I'm afraid I can't; I have to show you a letter."

"I suppose Rupert has been seeing Moona Chivvey again? Is that it?"

"Well, yes. But that's not all. Not a word to Madeline! Isn't it curious, Bertha, troubles about women are always the same. Either *they* want *you* to marry *them*, or *they* won't marry *you!*"

"Oh, really? Good-bye."

"How brilliant you're looking, Bertha! You've got your hair done in that mysterious new way again."

"How on *earth* can you know through the telephone?"

"Why, easily. By your voice. You talk in a different way—to suit it."

"Do I? How funny! Good-bye."

Ten minutes later Percy came in.

He seemed pleased to see his young brother.

"What's that book you've brought, Cliff?"

"It's 'The New Arabian Nights.'"

Percy laughed.

"Oh yes, I know—the copy I gave Bertha. Have you decided to let her have it back on mature consideration?"

"Oh, I say, Percy! Come off the roof; there's a good chap," said the boy, blushing a little.

"I think I shall have to take a holiday from chambers to-morrow," Percy said. "Shall we take him out to lunch, Bertha?"

"By all means; or, at any rate, you take him, Percy."

"Are you engaged in the morning?" he asked her very quickly.

"I ought to look in at my dressmaker's for a minute," she said, feeling angry with Nigel that he had made her promise to conceal even a few minutes of her day.

No more was said on the subject.

Presently, Percy went upstairs to his room and turned the key. He then took out of a drawer and placed in front of him, in their order, three rather curious-looking letters, written in typewriting on ordinary plain white notepaper. The first two, both of which began "*Dear Mr. Kellynch,*" were four pages long, and gave some information in somewhat mysterious terms. The third one had no beginning, and merely mentioned an hour and a place where, he was told, he would find his wife on the following morning, if he wished to do so, in the company of an individual with the initials N. H. The letter further advised him to go there and find her and take steps to put a stop to the proceedings which had been watched for some time by somebody who signed the letter "your true and reliable friend."

The right thing to do, according to all unwritten laws of the conduct of a gentleman, would be to destroy such communications and at once forget them. To show them to her, Percy felt, would be degrading to himself and to such a woman as his wife, whom he now realised he placed on a pedestal. The idea of seeing the pedestal rock seemed to take the earth from under his feet. But not only that, he now felt that, though he hadn't known it, he loved her, not with a mild, half-patronising affection, but with the maddening jealousy of a lover in the most passionate stage of love. A man placed in his position nearly always thinks that it is the idea of being deceived that hurts the most. Particularly when the object of suspicion is his wife. Now he knew it was not that; he could forgive the deception; but he couldn't bear to think that any other man could think of her from that point of view at all. And if he found that the mere facts stated in the three letters were true, even if the inferences suggested were utterly false, he had made up his mind what to do. He would go and see Nigel on the subject, forbid him the house, saying that too frequent visits had caused talk, and never mention the subject to Bertha. That was his present plan. Perhaps it would not be possible to carry it out, but that was his idea.

The fact that Bertha had been vague about her morning engagement—for it was really unlike her not to seem pleased at the idea of spending the whole day with him and the little brother—so agonised Percy that he pretended to have a headache and saw practically nothing of Bertha till the next day. He said then that he would go to chambers, meet Clifford at Prince's and come home after lunch and take Bertha out somewhere. This was to leave her perfectly free, so that she need not alter any arrangements. He wished to see what she would do.

It was a glorious morning, and Percy felt rather mean and miserable and unlike the day as he left the house.

Bertha was already dressed, looking deliciously fresh and pink, and sparkling and fair as the sunshine. A second of acute physical jealousy made him remark rather bitterly before he left that her hat was a little bit striking, wasn't it? Upon which she at once, in her good-tempered, amiable way (only too delighted that he should have noticed anything in her toilette even to object to it), plucked the white feather out of the black hat and put a little coat on over her dress, so as to look less noticeable.

At a quarter past eleven Percy paid his shilling at the gallery, walked in, looking slowly at the drawings on the walls in the narrow passage that led to the rooms.

The moment he reached the first door on the left-hand side, which was open, he saw through it, exactly opposite to him, seated on a sofa, Bertha, looking up and chattering to Nigel Hillier, who was looking down in a protecting manner, and listening with great interest to her conversation.

Neither of them saw him.

The pain of finding one part of the letter true was so startling and terrible that he dared not look another moment; a second more, and he might have made a scandal, perhaps for ever after to be regretted, and possibly entirely groundless.

He walked straight out of the gallery again, and drove to Sloane Street in a taxi. During the drive he felt extraordinary sensations. He remembered an occasion when he had been to a dentist as a little boy, and the strange new suffering it had caused him. Then he thought that when he got home, he would feel better. Instead of that the sight of the familiar house was unbearable agony; he could not endure to go into it; he drove back again to the club of which both he and Nigel were members, and where Nigel was generally to be found before lunch. There he tried to wait and master himself a little; it was peculiar torture to have left them there now. He felt he would like to go back to the gallery and at least spoil their morning. But that, his sound sense told him, would be a mistake. He would wait there till Nigel came in.

CHAPTER XII

A LOVE SCENE

PERCY waited on and on, minute after minute, half-hour after half-hour, reading the morning papers, staring with apparent deep interest at the pictures in the weekly journals—rather depressing foreshortened snapshots of society at racecourses. These people, caught unawares, seemed to be all feet and parasols, or smiles and muffs. Then, feeling rather exhausted, he ordered a drink, and forgot it, and smoked a cigarette. When he saw anyone he knew, he put on an absent-minded air, and avoided the friend's eye. He looked at his watch as if in sudden anxiety, and found that it was half-past one. This was the time he was to meet his little brother at Prince's. He made inquiries and found that Nigel was expected to lunch at the club. It was horrible! He could not leave the boy at the restaurant waiting for him, and he was not up to the mark either, at the moment, for seeing Nigel Hillier; he felt as if the top of his head had been smashed in. Yet his common-sense and reasoning power gradually prevailed over his emotion. And as he sat there, Percy changed his mind.

At first he had thought it would be cowardly to her to attack his wife on the subject; it was the man with whom he should quarrel. And now it seemed to him different. His point of view altered. It seemed only fair now to give Bertha herself a chance of explaining matters. Thinking of her fresh, frank expression that morning, and looking back, he began to have, by some sort of second sight, a vision of his own stupid injustice. No! he must have been wrong! Nigel may have been a scoundrel, or—anything—but it couldn't be Bertha's fault. She may have been imprudent, out of pure innocence; that was all.

He got up, and now he decided to take his brother out to lunch, and then go back and talk to Bertha.

During the noisy, crowded lunch at Prince's, which entertained the boy so much that there was no necessity for the elder brother to talk, Percy came to a firm decision.

He would never tell Bertha anything at all about the anonymous letters.

He would tell her that he had seen her this morning at the gallery—as if by accident; but he would frankly admit a jealousy, even a suspicion of Nigel.

He would ask Bertha in so many words not to see Nigel again.

If she would agree to this, and if she were as affectionate as formerly, what did the rest matter? The letters must have been slanders; who *could* have written them? But, after all, what did it matter? If Bertha consented to do as he asked, they were untrue, and that was everything. He and Bertha would drop Hillier, and he would put the whole horrible business behind him; he would wipe it out, and forget it. The mere thought of such joy made him tremble . . . it seemed too glorious to be real, and as they approached the house again he began to believe in it.

Clifford had thoroughly enjoyed himself. He felt quite grown-up as he parted with Percy at Sloane Street, and drove home, singing to himself the refrain of Pickering's favourite song: "How much wood would a woodchuck chuck, if a woodchuck would chuck wood?"

"Percy, what is the matter?" Bertha asked anxiously, as she looked at him.

He had gone through a great deal that morning and looked rather worn out. . . . He spoke in a lower voice than usual.

"Look here, Bertha," he said, "I have something to tell you."

She waited, then, at a pause, said, rather pathetically:

"Oh, Percy, do tell me what it is? I've felt so worried about you lately. You seem to be changed. . . . I have felt very pained and hurt. Tell me what it is."

Percy looked at her. She was looking sweet, anxious and sincere. She leant forward, holding out her little hand. . . . If this was not genuine, then nothing on earth ever could be!

"Tell me, Percy," she repeated, looking up at him, as he stood by the fire, with that little movement of her fair head that he used to say was like a canary.

Percy looked down at her; all his imposingness, all his air of importance, and his occasional tinge of pompousness, had entirely vanished. He was simple, angry and unhappy.

"I found I hadn't got to go to chambers early this morning after all, so I walked down Bond Street. I went into the Grosvenor Gallery. I saw you there. . . . It seemed very strange you hadn't told me. Why didn't you? Why didn't you? Bertha, don't tell me anything that isn't true!"

Her eyes sparkled. She stood up beaming radiant joy. She went to him impulsively; everything was all right; he was jealous!

"Oh, Percy! I can explain it all."

Hastily, eagerly, impulsively, with the most obvious honesty and frankness, she told him of how Nigel had promised to help her with Madeline, of how he had planned with her to make Madeline happy; she told him of the variable and unaccountable conduct of Rupert Denison to Madeline, of his marked attention at one moment, his coldness at another. Foolishly, she had been led to believe that Nigel could make things all right. Now this morning Nigel had asked her to meet him to tell her that Rupert had been seen choosing hats for another girl. Bertha was in doubt whether she ought to tell Madeline, and make her try and cure her devotion. And Bertha had thought it all the kinder of Nigel because his brother, Charlie, was very much in love with her.

Percy stopped her in the middle of the story. He could take no sort of interest in it at present. He was much too happy and relieved; he was in the seventh heaven.

"Yes . . . yes . . . all right, dear. Only you oughtn't to have made an appointment with him. Only promise that never again—— You see, things can be misconstrued. And, anyhow, I don't like to see you with Nigel Hillier. Frankly, I can't stand it. You'll make this sacrifice for me—if it is one, Bertha?"

He had quite decided to conceal all about the letters.

"Indeed, indeed I will; and I know I was wrong," she said. "I mean it's no good trying to help people too much. They must play their own game. You understand, don't you? Nigel was only to show me a letter he had written inviting the other girl to lunch—to take her away from Rupert. But it's all nonsense, and I'll have nothing more to do with it."

"Then that's all right," said Percy, sitting down, with a great sigh of relief.

"You didn't really think for a moment, seriously, that I ever—that I didn't—oh, you never stopped knowing how much I love you?" she asked, with tears in her eyes.

Percy said that he had not exactly thought that. Also, he was not jealous—that was not the word—he merely wished her to promise never to see or speak to Nigel again as long as they lived, and never to recognise him if she met him: that was all. He was perfectly reasonable.

"It's perhaps a little bit difficult in some ways, dearest. But I promise you faithfully to do my very, very best. And this I absolutely swear—I will never see him without your approving and knowing all about it. But as I shouldn't exactly like him to think you thought anything—I mean—I think you must leave it a little to me—to my tact, to get rid of him; and trust me. And I want you to know that I shouldn't care if I never saw him again. I don't even like him. And I really don't think he cares for me; I'm quite certain it's your fancy."

"Can you give me your word of honour that he never——"

"Never, by word or look," answered Bertha.

"That's all right," said Percy.

Bertha sat on the arm of his chair and leant her head against his shoulder.

At that moment he thought he had never known what happiness was before.

Then she said:

"It's all right now, then, Percy? That was all, and the cloud's gone?"

"Quite, absolutely," he answered, mentally tearing the letters into little bits.

Then she said:

"Percy, of course you never really thought . . . you never could think that I meant to deceive you in any way. . . . But supposing Nigel had had any treacherous ideas—let us say, supposing that Nigel, though he's married, and all that—suppose you found out that he had liked me, and wanted to spoil our happiness? . . . I mean, suppose you found out that he had been making love to me? . . . What would you have done?"

"I should have killed him," replied Percy. Could a man have said anything that would please a woman as much as this primitive assertion?

Bertha threw her arms round his neck. She was perfectly happy. He was in love with her.

CHAPTER XIII

RECONCILIATION

BERTHA decided it was better to curtail Nigel's visits and make them fewer gradually; she had quite convinced Percy of her sincerity, and he also had come to the conclusion that it would be foolish and *infra dig* to let the jealousy be suspected. He trusted her again now; and they were both deeply and intensely happy. Being ashamed of the letters, Percy said nothing about them; in a day or two he had come to the conclusion that he would leave it entirely to Bertha's tact.

"All I ask is," he said, "that you will see him as little and as seldom as you can, without making too much fuss about it, or letting him know what I thought."

"And I promise to do that," she said. "I long never to see him again. It's only on account of Madeline I wanted to have one more little talk with him—about her and Rupert. After that I'll manage without him, I assure you. I swear not to give him anything more to do for me. But what I can't understand, dear, is what put the idea into your head."

"Never mind. You were seeing him too often. And, remember, I know that he was in love with you once and wanted to marry you."

"But, dear boy, that was ten years ago, and he married somebody else."

"Which he may regret by now. Well, I trust all to your tact, Bertha."

"He's coming to-day," Bertha said. "And then I'm going to make him understand I no longer want his help."

"Right."

Percy went out, looking very happy. He did not forget to kiss her now, and he himself had sent the large basket of flowers that Nigel nearly fell over when he came in the afternoon.

"A new admirer?" asked Nigel.

"No, an old one. So you say that you met Rupert buying a hat for Miss Chivvey, and saw them the next day walking together, and she was wearing it."

"Yes. And, as I told you, I thought this rather serious, so I wrote and invited the young lady to lunch with me."

"Did she accept?"

"That is what I've come to tell you about to-day. She was engaged, but asked me to invite her another time."

"Exactly. Now, Nigel, I want to tell you something. I think I've been doing wrong intriguing for Madeline, and it hasn't been fair to her really. I've decided to tell her what you told me about Rupert, and then leave things to take their course. And I oughtn't to countenance asking the other girl to lunch. It was horrid of me—I'm ashamed of myself, both on account of her and of Mary. Don't do it; I'd rather not."

Nigel looked up at her sharply.

"Do these sudden and violent scruples mean simply that you don't want me any more?"

"A little," she replied.

"I've noticed you've seemed very cold and unkind to me the last week or so," he said. "You seem to be trying to change our relations."

"I don't see why we should have any relations," answered Bertha. "After all, I know instinctively that Mary doesn't like me."

"What in heaven's name does that matter?" he asked.

"A good deal to me."

There was a moment's silence.

Nigel looked surprised and more hurt than she would have expected. Then he said:

"All right, Bertha. I hope I can take a hint. I won't bother you any more. I won't try to help you in anything till you ask me."

She was silent.

Then he went on:

"Might I venture to ask whether you suspect I've been making the most of our plans for Madeline to see as much of you as I could?"

"Oh, I didn't say that."

"If you had, perhaps you would have been right," he said, but seeing her annoyed expression he changed his tone, and said:

"No, my dear, truly I only wanted to do a good turn for you and your friend. It's off now, that's all. I sha'n't interfere again."

He stood up.

She hesitated for one moment.

"Do you think Rupert has not been sincere with Madeline?"

"I can't say. I wouldn't go so far as that. I think he varies—likes the contrast between the two. But if he decides to marry, I don't think he'd propose to Miss Chivvey. Well, good-bye. I won't call again till you ask me."

Her look of obvious relief as she smilingly held out her hand piqued him into saying:

"I see you want your time to yourself more. Before I go, will you answer me one little question?"

"Of course I will."

He still held her hand. She took it away.

"What is the question?"

"Who sent you those flowers, Bertha?"

"Have you any right to ask?"

"I think so—as an old friend. They're compromisingly large, and there's a strange mixture of orchids and forget-me-nots, roses and gardenias that I don't quite like. It looks like somebody almost wildly lavish—not anxious to show off his taste, but sincerely throwing his whole soul into the basket."

She laughed, pleased.

"Who sent you the flowers, Bertha?"

He was standing up by the door.

"Percy," she answered.

"Oh!"

CHAPTER XIV

"TANGO"

MADELINE had taken the gossip about Rupert and Miss Chivvey very bravely, but very seriously. It pained her terribly, but she was grateful to Bertha for telling her.

A fortnight passed, during which she heard nothing from Rupert, and then one morning, the day after a dance, she called to see Bertha.

Percy had had no more anonymous letters, and Nigel had remained away. He was deeply grateful, for he supposed Bertha had managed with perfect tact to stop the talk without giving herself away, or making him ridiculous.

Bertha had never looked happier in her life. She was sitting smiling to herself, apparently in a dream, when her friend came in.

"Bertha," she said, "I have some news. I danced the tango with Nigel's brother Charlie last night, and at the end—he really does dance divinely—what do you think happened? I had gone there perfectly miserable, for I had seen and heard nothing of Mr. Denison except that one letter after the Ballet—and then Charlie proposed to me, and I accepted him, like in a book!"

Bertha took her hand.

"My dear Madeline, how delightful! This is what I've always wanted. It's so utterly satisfactory in every way."

"I know, and he is a darling boy. I was very frank with him, Bertha. I didn't say I was in love with him, and he said he would teach me to be."

"It's frightfully satisfactory," continued Bertha. "Tell me Madeline, what made you change like this?"

"Well, dear, I've been getting so unhappy: I feel Rupert has been simply playing with me. I heard the other day that *they* were dining out alone together—I mean Rupert and that girl. I don't blame him, Bertha. It was I, in a sense, who threw myself at his head. I admired and liked him and gradually let myself go and get silly about him. But this last week I've been pulling myself together and seeing how hopeless it was, and just as I'd begun to conquer my feeling—to fight it down—then this nice dear boy, so frank and straightforward and sincere, came along, and—oh! I thought I should like it. To stop at home with mother after my sort of disappointment seemed too flat and miserable: I couldn't bear it. Now I shall have an object in life. But, Bertha," continued Madeline, putting her head on her shoulder, "I've been absolutely frank, you know."

"I guessed you would be; it was like you. But I hope you didn't say too much to Charlie. It would be a pity to cloud his pleasure and spoil the sparkle of the fun. By the time you're choosing carpets together and receiving your third cruet-stand you will have forgotten such a person as Rupert Denison exists—except as a man who played a sort of character-part in the curtain-raiser of your existence."

"Well, I hope so. But I did tell Charlie I was not in love with him, and he said he would try to make me."

"I only hope that you're not doing it so that your mother should ask Rupert to the wedding? Not that I myself sha'n't enjoy that."

"Honestly, Bertha, I don't think so. More than anything it's because I want an object in life."

"Here's a letter from Nigel," said Bertha. "I expect he'll be making this an excuse to drop in again."

"Yes; but you mustn't tease Percy, because everything happened just as you wanted it to," said Madeline. "I really was surprised at how suddenly and determinedly Charlie began again. He had seemed almost to give me up. He dances the tango so beautifully; I think it all came through that. We got on so splendidly at tango teas. At any rate, but for that I shouldn't have seen him so often."

"It's a tango marriage," said Bertha.

Bertha strongly suspected a little manœuvring of Nigel's in the course of the last fortnight, but did not realise how much there had been of it. The day Bertha had practically said he was not to interfere any longer, Nigel thoroughly realised that Percy must be jealous. He was wildly annoyed at this, since it would be a great obstacle, besides proving Percy was in love, but he saw the urgency of falling in at once with her wish; not opposing it, being absolutely obedient to it. This was not the moment to push himself forward—to show his feelings. Tact and diplomacy must be used. Of course, he had not the faintest notion about Mary and her letters, but merely thought that a sudden relapse of conjugal affection on Percy's side—confound him!—and an attack of unwonted jealousy had made Percy say something to Bertha to cause her coldness.

He remained away, but he thought of more than one plan to regain the old intimacy.

Quite unscrupulously he played several little tricks, at least he made several remarks about one to the other, to make the apparently hesitating Rupert more interested in Miss Chivvey and less so in Madeline, while he urged his brother Charlie on, and insisted on his continuing his court. The result was quicker than he had expected, and after a very little diplomacy Charlie had found Madeline willing to accept him. As Madeline was to Bertha just like a sister, it was natural that they should meet again now, and in this letter Nigel asked permission to call and have a chat.

Bertha agreed, for although she was slightly on her guard against the possibility of his wishing to flirt, she had not the faintest idea, as I have said, of Nigel's determined resolve.

Nigel had been fairly unhappy of late. Caring very little for any of his other friends, and having this *idée fixe* about Bertha—which became much stronger at the opposition and the idea of Percy's jealousy—he moped a good deal and had spent more time than usual with Mary. Nigel was one of those very rare men, who are becoming rarer and rarer, who, having passed the age of thirty-five, still regard love as the principal object of life. That Nigel did so was what made him so immensely popular with women as a rule. Women feel instinctively when this is so, and the man who makes sport, ambition or art his first interest, and women, and romance in general, a mere secondary pleasure, is never regarded with nearly the same favour as the man who values women chiefly, even though that very man is naturally far less reliable in his affection and almost invariably deceives them. To be placed in the background of life is what the average woman dislikes the most; she would rather be of the first importance as a woman even if she knows she has many rivals.

Bertha was exceptional, in that she did not care for the Don Juan type of man, but was rather inclined to despise him. She would far rather have ambition, business, art, duty, any other object in life as her rival, than another woman.

Percy received no more of the singular typewritten letters. He kept those that he had locked up in a box. Mary had grown a little frightened at the apparent success of those she sent. She never heard anything about them, but she knew that Nigel had not been seeing Bertha since the note about the picture gallery. She began to be happier again. Nigel was a great deal more at home, though not more affectionate. And Mary was one of those women, by no means infrequent, who are fairly satisfied if they can, by hook or by crook, by any trick or any tyranny, keep the man they care for somehow under the same roof with them—if only his body is in the house, even if they know it is against his will, and that his soul is far away. She would far rather that his desire was elsewhere, if only *he* were positively present—the one dread, really, being that he should be enjoying himself with anyone else. Mary preferred a thousand times a silent, sulky evening with Nigel going up to his room about the same time that she went to hers, than, as he used to be when they were first married, gay, affectionate and caressing to her, and then going out. She would gladly make him a kind of prisoner, even at the cost of making him almost dislike her, rather than give him his freedom—even to please him—a freedom which included the possibility of his seeing Bertha again.

Although she was unjust and mistaken in her facts, it was, of course, a correct instinct that made her aware that Bertha was the great attraction—the one real object of passion in Nigel's life. But she was incapable of believing that Bertha did not care for him, that if she had she would never have flirted with the husband of another woman. Merely because Bertha was pretty and admired, Mary, with her strange narrow-minded bitterness, took it for granted that it was impossible that she could be also a delicately scrupulous, generous, and high-minded creature. But just as passion will make one singularly quick-sighted, it can also make one dense and stupid. Considering that Mary was madly in love with her own hushand, it was absurd she should suppose it impossible that Bertha should take the slightest interest in hers. Of course Mary had heard that they were very devoted—if she had not, what would have been the use of writing the letters?—but she chose to believe that it was only on the husband's side, and that Bertha must of necessity be, of course, sly and deceitful. She hated Bertha violently, and yet she was by nature the kindest of women; only this one mania of hers completely altered her, and made her bitter, wild, hard and unscrupulous, stupid and clever, cowardly and reckless. A woman's jealousy of another woman is always sufficiently dreadful, but when the object of jealousy is hers by legal right, when the sense of personal property is added to it, then it is one of the most terrible and unreasonable things in nature.

CHAPTER XV

CLIFFORD'S HISTORICAL PLAY

BERTHA was sitting with her little brother-in-law. She was to give him half-an-hour, after which she expected a visit from Nigel.

"What on earth is it, old boy?"

She saw he had some rather untidy papers in his hand and was looking extremely self-conscious, so she spoke kindly and encouragingly.

"Well, I daresay you noticed, Bertha, in my report, that history was very good."

"I think I did," she said gravely. "If I recollect right the report said: 'History nearly up to the level of the form.'"

"Oh, I say, was that all? Gracious! Well, anyhow, I've read a lot of history, and I'm fearfully keen about it. And, I say, my idea was, you see, I thought I'd write a historical play."

"Oh! what a splendid idea!" cried Bertha, jumping up, looking very pleased, but serious. "Have you got it there, Cliff?"

"Yes. Well, as a matter of fact, I have got a bit of it here."

"Are you going to let me read it?"

"Well, I don't think you can," he answered rather naïvely. "It's not quite clean enough; but I'll read a bit of it to you, if you don't mind. Er—you see—it's about Mary."

"Which Mary?"

"Oh, Bertha! what a question! As if I'd write about William and Mary, or—er—er—I beg your pardon—I mean the other Mary. No, Mary, Queen of Scots, is the only one who's any good for a play."

"Well, go on, Clifford."

"Well, it's a little about"—he spoke in a low, gruff voice—" at least partly about hawking. You know, the thing historical people used to do—on their wrists."

"Oh yes, I know, I know! I beg your pardon, Clifford."

"With birds, you know," he went on. "Oh, and I wanted to ask you, what time of the year *do* people hawk?"

"What time of the year? Oh, well, I should think almost any time, pretty well, whenever they liked, or whenever it was the fashion."

"I see." He made a note. "Well, I hope you won't be fearfully bored, Bertha."

"I say, Cliff, don't apologise so much. Get on with it."

"Well, you see, it's a scene at a country inn to begin with."

"Ah, I see. Yes, it would be," she murmured.

"At a country inn, and this is how it begins. It's at a country inn, you see. 'Scene: a country inn. The mistress of the inn, a buxom-looking woman of middle age, is being busy about the inn. It is a country inn. She is making up the fire, polishing tankards, etc., drawing ale, etc. On extreme L. of stage is seated, near a tankard, a youth of some nineteen summers, who is sitting facing the audience, chin dropped, and apparently wrapped in thought.'"

"Excuse me a moment, old chap, but that sounds as if his chin was wrapped in thought."

"So it does; I'll change that. Thanks awfully for telling me, Bertha."

"Not at all, dear."

"But it is frightfully decent of you."

"All right. Get on."

"'At the back of the stage R. are seated two men; one of some eight and twenty summers the other of some six and twenty years old. They are seated in the corners of the stage and in apparently earnest conversation.' (Now the dialogue begins, Bertha, listen):

"'YOUTH: Are you there, mistress? Is my ale nigh on ready? Zounds, I'm mighty thirsty, I am.

"'MISTRESS: Ay, ay, great Scot! here's your ale. You can't expect to be served before the quality.'"

"What did Pickering think of this?" interrupted Bertha.

"Pickering! Oh! I wouldn't show it to a chap like that. At any rate, not unless you think it's all right, Bertha."

"Why, my dear boy, you'd better tell me the plot, I think, before you read me any more."

"Mr. Nigel Hillier," announced the servant.

Nigel sprang brightly in (just a little agitated though he managed to hide it), Bertha took her toes off the sofa, Clifford took up his play and shoved it into his pocket with a slight scowl.

CHAPTER XVI

A SECOND PROPOSAL

THE day after Madeline's engagement two letters were handed to her. One in Charlie's handwriting, short and affectionate; full of the exuberance of the newly affianced, touchingly happy. The other one she opened, feeling somewhat moved, as she recognised the handwriting of Rupert Denison. To her utter astonishment she found it was four sheets of his exquisite little handwriting, and it began thus:

"MY DEAR, MY VERY DEAR MADELINE,—The last note I had from you—now nearly a month ago—came to me like a gift of silver roses. I did not answer it, but during the dark days in which I have not seen you, I have been learning to know myself. You wondered, perhaps, how I was occupied, why you did not hear from me again—at least I hope you did. ("I didn't, for I knew only too well," Madeline murmured to herself.) Now I have learnt to understand myself. Sometimes almost inhumanly poetic you have seemed to me, and others; when I remembered your simple refined beauty you suggested the homelike atmosphere that is my dream."

She started and went on reading.

"Madeline, do you understand, all this time, though perhaps I hardly knew it myself, I loved you. I love you and shall never change. It is my instinct to adore the admirable, and I know now that you are the most adorable of creatures. No words can describe your wonderfulness, so I send you my heart instead.

"I think, dear, our life together will be a very beautiful one. It will be a great joy to me to lead you into beautiful paths. How glad I shall be to see the bright look of your eyes, when you greet me after this letter! What a perfect companion you will be! Write at once. I have much more to say when we meet. When shall this be? Your ever devoted and idolising

"RUPERT.

"*P.S.*—I propose not to make our engagement public quite yet, but to keep our happiness to ourselves for a few weeks, and be married towards the end of the summer. What do you say, my precious Madeline?"

Madeline was at once delighted and horrified. How characteristic the letter was! Why had she not waited? There was no doubt about it, she had made a mistake. Rupert was the man she loved—notwithstanding his taking everything so for granted. Charlie must be sacrificed. But she must tell Rupert what had happened, of course.

After sending a telegram to Rupert asking him to meet her at a picture gallery, for she could not bear asking him to call until everything was settled up, the bewildered girl rushed off to see Bertha.

Bertha took in the situation at once. Madeline had only accepted Charlie in despair, thinking and believing that Rupert cared for another girl. It was madness, equally unfair to herself and to Charlie, to go on with the marriage now. Bertha quite agreed, though she grieved for the boy, and regretted how things had turned. . . . But, after all, Madeline cared for Rupert and she could not be expected to throw away her happiness now it was offered to her.

Bertha advised complete frankness all round. The only thing at which she hesitated a little was Madeline's intention of telling of her engagement to Rupert. She feared a little the effect on the complicated subtlety of that conscientious young man. . . . However, it was to be.

Fortunately no one as yet knew of the engagement except the very nearest relatives. Madeline's mother would only regret bitterly that Madeline could not accept them both, it being very rare nowadays for two agreeable and eligible young men to propose to one girl in two days.

Nigel was furious and had no patience with these choppings and changings, as he called them.

Charlie took it bravely and wrote Madeline a very generous and noble letter, which touched her, but it did not alter her intention. She had just received it when she went to meet Rupert.

The day which had dragged on with extraordinary excitement and with what seemed curious length had just declined in that hour between six and seven when the vitality seems to become somewhat lowered; when it is neither day nor evening, the stimulation of tea is over and one has not begun to dress for dinner.

At this strange moment Madeline burst in again on Bertha and said:

"Bertha, isn't it terrible! I've told him everything and he refuses me. He's sent me back. He says if I'm engaged to Charlie it's my duty to marry him. He's fearfully hurt with me and shocked at my conduct to Charlie. Oh, it's too dreadful; I'm heartbroken!"

"Oh, what an irritating creature!" cried Bertha. "It's just the sort of thing he would do. I'd better see him at once, Madeline."

"You can't; he's going to Venice to-night," said Madeline, and burst into tears.

CHAPTER XVII

MORE ABOUT RUPERT

RUPERT had gone through a great many changes during the last few weeks. He had begun to grow rather captivated by Miss Chivvey and in his efforts to polish, refine and educate her had become rather carried away himself. But towards the end she began to show signs of rebellion; she was bored, though impressed. He took her to a serious play and explained it all the time, during which she openly yawned. Finally, when she insisted on his seeing a statuette made of her by her artistic friend, an ignorant, pretentious little creature, known as Mimsie, they positively had a quarrel.

"Well, I don't care what you say; I think it's very pretty," when Rupert pointed out faults that a child could easily have seen.

"So it may be, my dear child—not that I think it is. But it's absolutely without merit; it's very very bad. It could hardly be worse. If she went all over London I doubt if she could find a more ridiculous thing calling itself a work of art. Can't you see it's like those little figures they used to have on old-fashioned Twelfth Cakes, made of sugar."

"No, I can't. Shut up! I mayn't know quite so much as you, but ever since I was a child everybody's always said I was very artistic."

They were sitting in her mother's drawing-room in Camden Hill. Rupert glanced round it: it was a deplorable example of misdirected aims and mistaken ambitions; a few yards of beaded curtains which separated it from another room gratified Moona with the satisfactory sensation that her surroundings were Oriental. As a matter of fact, the decoration was so commonplace and vulgar that to attempt to describe it would be painful to the writer whilst having no sort of effect on the reader, since it was almost indescribable. From the decorative point of view, the room was the most unmeaning of failures, the most complete of disasters.

Rupert had hoped, nevertheless, to cultivate her taste, and educate her generally. He was most anxious of all to explain to her that, so far from being artistic, she was the most pretentious of little Philistines. Why, indeed, should she be anything else? It was the most irritating absurdity that she should think she was, or wish to be.

Rupert was growing weary of this, and beginning to think his object was hopeless.

A certain amount of excitement that she had created in him by her brusque rudeness, her high spirits, even the jarring of her loud laugh, was beginning to lose its effect; or rather the effect was changed. Instead of attracting, it irritated him.

About another small subject they had a quarrel—she was beginning to order him about, to regard him as her young man, her property—and was getting accustomed to what had surprised her at first—that he didn't make love to her. She had ordered him to take her somewhere and he had refused on the ground that he wanted to stop at home and think!

She let herself go, and when Moona Chivvey lost her temper it was not easily forgotten. She insulted him, called him a blighter, a silly ass, a mass of affectation.

He accepted it with gallant irony, bowing with a chivalrous humility that drove her nearly mad, but he never spoke to her again.

Perhaps nothing less than this violent scene would have shaken Rupert into examining his own feelings, and with a tremendous rebound he saw that he was in love with Madeline, and decided to marry her at once. How delighted the dear child would be!

He had seen very little of her lately, and he appreciated her all the more.

In her was genuine desire for culture; longing to learn; real refinement and intelligence, charm and grace, if not exactly beauty. Ah, those sweet, sincere brown eyes! Rupert would live to see her all she should be, and there was not the slightest doubt about her happiness with him. It never occurred to him for a single moment that anyone else could have been trying to take his place. Far less still that she should have thought of listening to any other man on earth but himself. When she came and told him all that had happened, the shock was great. He had never cared for her so much. But he declined to allow her to break her engagement; she could not play fast and loose with this unfortunate young man, Charlie Hillier, and although she declared, with tears, that she should break it off in any case, and never see him again, Rupert kept to his resolution, and started for Paris that night.

In answer to one more passionate and pathetic letter from her, he consented to write to her as a friend in a fortnight, but he said she must have known her own mind when she accepted Charlie.

Rupert clearly felt that he had been very badly treated; he said he never would have thought it of her; it was practically treachery.

When he went away he felt very tired, and had had enough, for the present, at any rate, of all girls and their instruction. Girls were fools.

He looked forward to the soothing consolations of the gaieties of Paris. He was not the first to believe that he could leave all his troubles and tribulations this side of the Channel.

CHAPTER XVIII

"A SPECIAL FAVOUR"

"I ADMIRE Madeline's conduct very much. I think it was splendid how she stood up to all the reproaches, and even ridicule; she told me that she had once, and only once, in her life been untrue to herself (she meant in accepting Charlie), and since then she has spoken the absolute truth to everybody about it all. She has been very plucky, and very straightforward, and only good can come of it. Honesty and pluck, especially for a girl—it's made so difficult for girls—they're the finest things in the world, *I* think."

Bertha was speaking to Nigel.

He had remained away for what seemed to him an extraordinarily long time. He was afraid that she was slipping out of his life, without even noticing it. Stopping away until she missed him was a complete failure, since she *didn't* miss him. And the day was approaching for the party Mary had consented to give.

He knew that Bertha had accepted but was afraid she didn't mean to come. That would be too sickening! To have all that worry with Mary, all that silly trouble and fuss for a foolish entertainment that he detested, all for nothing at all! And Mary was secretly enjoying the fact that she felt absolutely certain Percy would never let her come to Nigel's house. She did not suppose Percy had guessed the writer of the letters; but he must have thought his wife was talked about, and some effect certainly they had had; for in the last few weeks, she happened to know for a fact, Nigel had neither called on or met Mrs. Kellynch. This afternoon she knew nothing of, for her suspicions were beginning to fade, and she was not, at present, having him followed. Nigel had taken his chance and dropped in to tea and found luck was on his side—Bertha had just come in from a drive with Madeline.

"It's all very well," he answered, "to say you admire her conduct, her bravery, and all that! Whom had she to fight against? Only her mother, whom she isn't a bit afraid of, and Charlie, who, poor chap, is more afraid of her. The engagement wasn't even public before she broke it off."

"Yes; but, Nigel, it was very frank of her to tell everything so openly to Charlie. And now, poor girl, she's very unhappy, but very courageous—she's absolutely resolved never to marry. She says she's lost her Rupert by her own faults, and it serves her right."

"And suppose Rupert goes teaching English to an Italian girl at Venice, or gives her history lessons, or anything? Now he's once thought of marrying, he may marry his third pupil. Wouldn't Charlie have a chance then?"

"Never, unfortunately," Bertha replied.

"Do you think she'd wait on the chance that Rupert might have a divorce?"

"Nigel, how horrid you are to sneer like that. You never appreciated Madeline!"

"I think I did, my dear, considering I was especially keen on her marrying my brother, even when I knew she liked somebody else."

"Oh, that was only for him."

"Or, perhaps, do you think a little for me? I might have felt if my brother married your greatest friend that we were sort of relations," he said, with a laugh.

Bertha glanced at the clock.

"You can't send me away just this minute," he said. "You like honesty and frankness, and I've honestly come to ask you—are you coming to my party?"

Bertha paused a moment.

"Why?" she said. "Do you very particularly want me to?"

"Very. And I'll tell you the reason. It's to please Mary."

"Why should Mary care?"

"Bertha, I give you my word that she'll be terribly disappointed and offended if you don't. And"—he waited a moment—"I hardly know how to explain—it'll do me harm if you don't come—you and Percy. I can't exactly explain. Do me this good turn, Bertha. A special favour, won't you?"

He was artfully trying to suggest what he supposed to be the exact contrary to the fact. He knew Mary would be wild with joy if Bertha did not come, though he had no idea how extremely astonished and furious she would be if she should arrive, considering she had accepted. Of course in reality Mary thought nothing of the acceptance. She was both certain and determined that her "door would not be darkened" by Bertha's presence.

Bertha had not intended to go since she saw Percy's pleasure and relief at the cessation of the intimacy. But now? After all, Percy couldn't mind going in with her for a few minutes if she begged him.

"If you tell me it'll do you a good turn, Nigel—but I don't understand!"

"Do you wish me to explain?"

"No, I don't. I'll take your word. But all the more I don't want you to be always calling. I'm afraid Mary doesn't like me."

"It isn't that exactly."

Bertha thought of her own happiness with Percy. Her warm, kind heart made her say gently:

"Nigel, I hope you're nice and considerate to Mary? You make her happy?"

"Doesn't this look like it?" he answered. "She'll be in a state if you don't turn up." He sighed. "I've never said a word about it, but she's rather trying and tiresome if you want to know."

"Then I'm very, very sorry for her," said Bertha, "and you can't do enough for her. . . . Why, with those lovely children I'm sure she'd be ideally happy if——"

"Oh, you think, of course, it's my fault. It never occurs to you whether I'm happy!"

A look from her which she tried to repress reminded him of his deliberate choice. He thought the time had come to make her a little sorry for him, knowing her extreme tenderness of heart. He spoke in a lower voice, and looked away.

"If I'm sometimes a bit miserable, it serves me right."

"Be good to her," said Bertha.

"I'll do anything on earth you'll tell me."

"What are the children's names?"

"Nigel and Marjorie."

"Darling pets, I suppose?"

"Isn't it extraordinary, Bertha," he said. "I've no right to say it to you, but that's my great trouble."

"What?"

"She doesn't care much about them."

"I don't believe it," said Bertha, shaking her head. "It's you who are mistaken."

"Am I?"

"Nigel, remember, I know you pretty well."

"And you think I'm trying to make you sorry for me?"

"I won't say that. But you ought to be happy, and so ought your wife."

He spoke in a different tone, with his usual cheery smile.

"Well, if you will grace our entertainment, I promise we will be happy. Do come, Bertha!" He was taking all this trouble simply so as not to have a boring evening at his own home!

"Very well, Nigel," she answered, with a kind, frank smile. "I'll come. Lately Percy's had so much work that in the evenings he hasn't been very keen on going out to parties."

"And you don't go without him?" he asked with curiosity.

"No. Aren't I unfashionable?"

"You're delightful."

"Good-bye," she said, holding out her hand.

He took it, and held it, saying:

"And now I sha'n't see you again until a few minutes at the party, and heaven knows when after that."

"I'll bring Madeline. Shall I?"

"Oh yes, do. It'll be *some* party, as the Americans say, and Charlie won't be there."

"Good-bye again."

"What are you going to wear?" he asked, in his old, brotherly voice, lingering by the door.

"Salmon-coloured chiffon with a mayonnaise sash," she answered, fairly pushing him out of the room. "Do go."

CHAPTER XIX

A DEVOTED WIFE

TO anyone who knew Percy Kellynch and his wife, it would have been a matter of some surprise to observe the extreme enthusiasm and devotion that she showed for him. He was an excellent fellow, and had many good qualities, but he was not mentally by any means anything at all extraordinary; she was a very much more highly organised being in every possible way than he was. Percy was exceedingly kind and straight, yet there were, doubtless, many thousands of men exactly like him in England. In his rather simple and commonplace point of view he was, perhaps more like an ordinary English soldier than a barrister. He did not worship false gods, but, not being a soldier, and having perhaps learnt more of life in some respects than they generally do, he was inclined to be rather surprised at his own cleverness. In a quiet way he had a high opinion of himself. He had been disposed to be a superior young man at twenty, and now, at thirty, he was not without a tinge of self-satisfaction, even pompousness. That his quickly discerning, subtle little wife should like and appreciate his good qualities; that she should, being of an affectionate nature, value him, was not surprising; but that, with her sense of humour and remarkable quickness, even depth of intellect, she should absolutely worship and adore him—for it amounted to that—was rather a matter of astonishment. But it must be remembered that her first love, Nigel Hillier, when she was eighteen, was, obviously, just exactly what one would have expected to dazzle her—quick, lively, fascinating and witty—this early romance had been a terrible disappointment. Bertha had bravely been prepared to wait for years, or to marry him on the moment; she had not the faintest idea that the money difficulties would be used to put an end to it on *his* side. When he had broken it off, saying that he feared her father was right, and that it was for her sake, she was terribly pained, seeing at once that his love was not of the same quality as hers. But when, in less than a week after that, he told her of his other engagement, it very nearly broke her heart, as the phrase goes. Yet she cured herself; and considering how young she was, she had an astonishing power of self-control; she was almost cured of her love, if not her grief, in a fortnight! She accepted Percy at the time without romance, though with a great liking, and looking up to him with a certain trust, but very soon the good qualities, in which he differed so remarkably from Nigel, and even the points in which he was deficient and in which Nigel excelled, made her care for him more. As the years went on, Bertha, who could do nothing by halves, began to adore Percy more and more. She thought absolutely nothing of Nigel at all, so very little that she had let him dangle about without a thought of the past, being under the impression that he was contented in his married life. When he began again to find excuses to see her, and to start a sort of friendship, she did not discourage it, for the very reason that she wanted him to see that chapter in her life was absolutely closed and forgotten.

His extreme desire that she should come to their entertainment, his various implications—that Mary should think there was something in it if she didn't come—then this new suggestion that he was not happy at home, and, on looking back, Percy's extraordinary behaviour, suddenly made her see things in a different light. She saw that Nigel probably now imagined himself in love with her, and that it was not entirely Percy's imagination; that it was even more necessary than she had thought to put an end to the friendship. It made her furious when she thought of it—the selfishness, the treachery—meanly to throw her over because Mary was rich, and afterwards to try and come back and spoil both their homes in amusing himself by a romance with her. Even if Bertha had not cared for her husband, Nigel would have been the very last man in the world she could have looked upon from that point of view. Amusing as he was, she never thought of him without a slightly contemptuous smile. And she loved Percy so very much; he was so entirely without self-interest: he might have a certain amount of harmless vanity, but he was purely unworldly, generous, broadminded and good, and his own advantage was the very last thing that ever entered his head.

Until the trouble about Nigel she had feared he was growing cold, but Percy's conduct on that subject had thoroughly satisfied her. He had been very jealous but kind to her: he trusted and believed in her when she was frank, and he certainly seemed more in love with her than ever. Percy was so reliable, so true and *real*. She took up the dignified, charmingly flattered photograph of him. . . .

What a noble forehead! What a beautiful figure he had! And though he seemed so calm and so cold, he was passionate and could be violent. His intellect was not above the average, but his power of emotion most certainly was. . . . Dear Percy!

And now she had promised to go to Nigel's house, she would get Percy to agree that evening.

Bertha told him of Nigel's visit, and of the request.

He frowned.

"You've accepted, and that's enough. I suppose you had to say you were going. You can easily write Mrs. Hillier an excuse the next day. Dozens of people will do it."

"Percy, I want to go."

He looked up angrily and in surprise.

"You want to go? You certainly can't. I don't wish it. Why, remember what you promised. Is this infernal intimacy beginning again?"

"Percy, to-day is only the third time I've seen him since we talked about it! And I hadn't the faintest idea he was coming to-day. I was surprised and annoyed to see him. Since Madeline broke it off with Charlie, we've heard nothing about them. Don't you believe me?"

"Naturally, I do. But it's a very odd thing a man should call here, and beg you to promise to come to his wife's party! Isn't it?"

"Perhaps it is. We stopped seeing him so suddenly, you see."

"What's that got to do with it?" said Percy, with angry impatience. The typewritten letters were torturing him. He had long been ashamed of not having shown them to Bertha, and made a clean breast of it. It was another reason why he hated Nigel and wanted the whole subject absolutely put aside and forgotten.

"In my opinion it suggests a very curious relation his coming here to-day like this. Not on your side, dear," he continued gently, putting his hand on hers. "But, if you don't mind my saying so, you don't know very much of the world, dear little Bertha, and in your innocence you are liable to be imprudent."

This was Percy's mistaken view of Bertha, but she did not dislike it. She was so determined now to be completely open that she did not try to put him off, and said candidly:

"It may be perfectly true that he's rather more anxious for me to be at the party than he need be. But, after all, there's not much harm in that, Percy. All I want is to go in with you for twenty minutes or half-an-hour, and then go away quite quickly. After that, if you like,

I'll give you my word of honour not to see him again."

"What's the object of it? No, I'm hanged if I go to that man's house."

"I promised as a special favour that I'd go."

"But what's the reason? Why is he so desperate you should be seen there?"

Percy frowned and thought a moment.

"Has his wife—do you think it's been noticed he doesn't come here so often?"

"It may have been. He didn't say so."

"Then it's damned impertinence of him to dare to come and ask you. Why should I take you there to make things comfortable with him and his wife?"

"Oh, Percy!"

"I don't want to have anything to do with them," Percy repeated, frowning angrily at her.

She paused and said sweetly:

"Don't look worried, darling. Won't you anyhow think it over for a day or two?"

Percy thought. He was a lawyer and it struck him that if the letters were to be really ignored it might be better for them to go in and be seen at the party, and if Bertha promised never to see him again, he knew she was telling the truth. But it was hard; it jarred on him.

"We'll leave the subject for a few days, Bertha," he said. "I'll think it over. But what I decide then must be final."

"Very well, Percy. . . . I've got *such* a lovely new dress! Pale primrose colour."

"The dress I saw you trying on? The canary dress?"

"Yes."

"No. I'm hanged if you'll wear that there!" he exclaimed.

Bertha went into fits of laughter.

"Oh, Percy, *how* sweet of you to say that! You're becoming a regular jealous husband, do you know? Darling! How delightful!"

CHAPTER XX

RUPERT AGAIN

AFTER the first reaction, Rupert felt, of course, to a certain extent, relieved and grateful to think that he was not engaged to Madeline. Undoubtedly, had he cared for her as she did for him, he would not have declined to marry her because of her accepting Charlie, more or less out of pique, or in despair. Yet, after having once really proposed he felt his emotions stirred, and almost as soon as he had sent her back (so to speak) to Charlie, he began to regret it—he began to be unhappy. *Au fond* he knew she would break it off with Charlie now, and would wait vaguely in hope for him. At first to recover from the intense annoyance of the whole thing, he thought he would, before Venice, go in a little for the gaieties of Paris. Rupert was still young enough to believe that the things presented to him as gaiety must necessarily be gay. A certain delicacy prevented his telling Madeline this now; though formerly when he had been to Paris, especially when he had had no intention of accepting any Parisian opportunities of amusement, he had often rubbed it in to her about the dazzling and dangerous charms of the gay city's dissipations, at which she was suitably impressed. But a nicer feeling made him now wish her to think of him as gliding down the lagoons of Venice, and dreaming of what might have been.

Madeline herself was really entirely without hope. She was certain she had lost all the prestige that she had had in his eyes; and she thought that she thoroughly deserved what had happened. She resolved to remain unmarried, and try to do good. Though she was hurt, and thought it showed how much less was Rupert's love than hers, still she respected him and admired him all the more for refusing to take her after accepting Charlie. She did not see that Rupert was a little too serious to be taken quite seriously.

Her mother added immensely to her depression. Mrs. Irwin was a woman who detested facts, so much so that she thought statistics positively indecent (though she would never have used the expression). When she was told there were more women than men in England, she would bite her lips and change the subject. She had had all the Victorian intense desire to see her daughter married young, and all the Victorian almost absurd delicacy in pretending she didn't. When, in one week, her only daughter—a girl who was not remarkably pretty, and had only a little money—should have proposals from no less than two attractive and eligible young men and should have muddled it up so badly that, though she had been prepared to accept both of them, she was now unable to marry either, her mother was, naturally, pained and disgusted.

Madeline, who was usually gentle and amiable to her, in this case spoke with a violence and determination that left no possible hope of her returning to Charlie Hillier. She left Mrs. Irwin nothing to do but to put on an air of refined resignation, of having neuralgia, which she now called neuritis, because Madeline had annoyed her so much, and of behaving, when Madeline sat with her, as much as possible like a person who was somewhere else.

Bertha was Madeline's only consolation and resource. Bertha took life with such delightful coolness.

"How would you advise me to behave to him, if it *had* come off—I mean if I *had* married Rupert?" Madeline asked Bertha.

She was fond of these problematical speculations.

"I should say be an angel, if he deserved it, or a devil if he appreciated it. Then—now and then—be non-existent, charming and indifferent, when you wanted to hedge—when there was no particular response. You'll go with me to the Hilliers' party, won't you, as Charlie will be away?"

"Of course I will—if you like. But will Percy go—and let you go?"

"He says he won't, but I think he will," she replied.

CHAPTER XXI

THE HILLIERS' ENTERTAINMENT

NO more had been said between them about the Hilliers' party; and Percy began to hope that it would be dropped. But on the morning Bertha asked him if he would like to take her out to dinner first with Madeline; assuming that, as he had said no more about it, he intended to go.

With those letters upstairs in the box, how could he?

"I simply can't," he answered. "I don't wish to go to that man's house."

"Then must I take Madeline alone?" said Bertha. "In all these years, Percy, I don't think I've ever been to a party without you."

"And I don't see why you should begin now," he answered.

"But, Percy, I want to go. Only for a few minutes."

"I'd much rather you didn't."

Bertha thought this tyrannical. She had promised Nigel, because he had implied to her that it would get him out of the domestic difficulty.

"Oh, do, Percy dear. It's treating me as if you didn't trust me. After all . . . if you like I'll swear to arrange never to see Nigel again."

"I wish you would."

"It's only because I think it would look marked."

Percy thought there was something in that, and he didn't dislike the idea of proving to the person, whoever it was, that had written the letters, how little effect they had had. Yet, they had left a tinge of jealousy that would easily be roused again, especially at her insistence. He noticed that she didn't make the fact that she was chaperoning Madeline an excuse, as most women would have done. She was frank about it. Still, he tried once more.

"I don't want you to go."

"But I want to."

She was not particularly fond of opposition, and began to look annoyed. She thought Percy was beginning to sit on her a little too much.

"Well," he said, "I shall not dine out with you and Madeline first: I don't care to. But I'll hire an electric motor for you at eleven, and it shall fetch you at twelve-thirty. If

Madeline doesn't want to come then, she can easily go back alone. It isn't far for her."

"Oh, she won't want to stop any longer than that."

"Oh, very well, we'll leave it like that. I shall dine at the club."

"It's unkind of you. I believe you don't want to see me start."

"You're quite right. I hate the idea of your appearing there in your lovely new dress. I suppose you want to wear it?"

"Oh, I don't care in the least," she answered, "if you'd rather not."

"Oh, hang it! Wear what you like," he answered rather crossly.

She did not see him again before she started, and, naturally, being a woman, she put on the new dress.

It was pale yellow, and she knew Percy would have liked it and would have called her a canary.

She went out, not in the best of tempers, and Madeline also, though looking very charming, did not look forward to the entertainment, and was thinking, with rather an aching heart, of Rupert in the lagoons of Venice.

The Hilliers' house was arranged with the utmost gorgeousness. Nigel felt a little return of his pride in it to-night. It was covered all over with rambler roses, and looked magnificent. There was such a crowd that Nigel hoped to get a little talk alone with Bertha, but feared she would not come. He was agreeably surprised to see her arrive alone with Madeline.

It so happened that Mary was not in the room when they were announced, and very soon Nigel managed to take her down, first into the refreshment-room, and then into the boudoir, which had been arranged with draperies and shaded lights.

"I just want to have a few words with you," he said, and got her into a little corner.

There was a heavy scent of roses; the music sounded faintly.

"Bertha!" he said. "It was too sweet of you to come. I shall never forget it. You don't know how miserable I am."

"Oh, rubbish!" she answered. "You've no earthly reason to be. I wish you wouldn't talk nonsense."

"I've never seen you look so lovely."

"I shall go away if you talk like that. Can't you see I don't like it?"

"I wonder Percy allowed you to come alone, looking like that."

"I came because I promised," she said. "You made me think, in some mysterious way, it would be a good thing for you. But after what you said about Mary, I want this to be distinctly understood: you are not to come and see me any more. Nothing in the world I should loathe so much as to be the cause of any trouble."

"Oh, my dear, but that you never could," he answered quickly.

"I hope not, and I'm not going to risk it. You chose your life, Nigel, and you have every reason to be happy."

"Have I? You don't know."

"Think of your children. I haven't got that pleasure, and yet I'm happy."

"Are you madly in love with Percy?" he asked, with a smile.

"Yes, I am," she answered.

At this moment a small crowd of people came in at the door. Mary, who was with them, looked hurriedly round the room, and seeing Bertha and Nigel in the corner, called him, taking no notice of her.

Bertha half rose, intending to go and shake hands with her, and Nigel quickly went to meet her, but Bertha paused, thinking Mary looked strange. She was very pale, and the white dress she wore made her look paler against her dull red hair. She wore a tiara, which seemed a little crooked, and her hair was disarranged. She was pale and trembling, but spoke in a loud voice that Bertha could hear. Within two yards of her, she said to Nigel, gesticulating with a feather fan:

"If you don't make that woman go away at once, I shall make a public scene!"

Bertha started up and looked at her in astonishment.

Mary, glaring at her, and still talking loudly, allowed Nigel to lead her out of the room.

He then came back.

"I think my wife's gone mad! Forgive her. She's ill, or something."

"I'm going now at once," said Bertha calmly. "Have a cab called for me, and let Madeline know that the motor will be here for her at half-past twelve. Leave me now—I don't want anything."

"For God's sake forgive me. She's off her head," said Nigel incoherently.

At her wish he ran upstairs.

Bertha got her cloak, and telling a friend she met that she was going on to a dance, she got into a taxi and went home.

CHAPTER XXII

BERTHA AT HOME

BERTHA drove back, furiously angry, principally with Nigel, whom she also pitied a little. It could be no joke to live with a woman like his wife. But he should not have deceived Bertha; he should have let her know; he should not have induced her to come against Percy's wish, at the risk of being insulted.

She was not anxious about Madeline, knowing that that sensible young lady would go to her own home when the carriage came, and that she could explain matters to her the next morning. Madeline was not *une faiseuse d'embarras.*

Bertha had brought her key as Percy had promised to wait up for her; the servants were to be allowed to go to bed. It was not long after twelve; she saw a light in the library and went in, fully intending to tell Percy everything.

She found him sitting by the fire, with a book. He had fallen asleep. She watched him for some moments, and she thought he looked pale and a little worried. . . . How wilful, how foolish it had been of her to go to the party without him! What did it matter? How trivial to insist on her own way! How ungrateful! For lately Percy had been devoted. And how lucky she was that he should care for her so much, after all these years.

As Bertha watched, she felt that strange suffering which is always the other side of intense love—the reverse of the medal of the ecstasy of passion—and she thought she would tell him nothing about it. Why should he be hurt, annoyed, and humiliated? It would spoil all the pleasure of her coming back so early—the unexpected delightful time they might have. . . . In this Bertha committed an error of judgment, for she forgot that he would probably hear of the scene some time or other, and would attach more importance to it than if she told him now.

"Percy," she whispered.

He woke up.

"You already! Why, it's only twelve o'clock! Oh, dear, how good of you to come so early."

"I didn't enjoy myself a bit," she murmured. "I'll never go out without you again. Do forgive me for going!"

"How is it you didn't enjoy it?"

"Because you hadn't seen me in my new dress. Do I look like a canary?"

"No," he said. "Let me look at you. No, you're not a canary—you're a Bird of Paradise."

CHAPTER XXIII

NIGEL'S LETTER

NEXT morning, as Bertha expected, Madeline came round to see her early. She brought with her a note. She said that Nigel had implored her to give it to her friend from him. He had put Madeline in the carriage, and had seemed greatly distressed. He told the girl that his wife had been ill lately and was not quite herself, and he feared she had offended Bertha.

"She certainly behaved like a lunatic," Bertha said, as she took the letter.

"Did you tell Percy?"

"As a matter of fact, no."

"Didn't he wonder at your coming home so early?"

"I'm afraid I pretended I rushed back to please him. Was it wrong of me? I'm afraid it was."

"I believe in frankness with people you can trust. And remember, quite a little while ago, Bertha, you were worried and depressed because you thought Percy was becoming a little casual and like an ordinary husband, and now, you naughty child, that he's been so *empressé* and affectionate, and jealous and attentive and everything that you like—now you first insist on going to a party when he doesn't wish it, and then you come home and tell him stories about it."

"I'm afraid I was wrong; but it was to spare him annoyance. Besides, I daresay I was weak. It was so delightful giving him a pleasant surprise."

She read the letter.

"Forgive me for asking your friend to give you this note—I only did it because I feared in writing to you to refer to what happened. Is it asking too much, Bertha, to beg you not to resent it? Not to hate me for to-night? Think of my shame and misery about it—to think I had pressed and begged you to come to be insulted in my house. You see now what I have tried to conceal. I am utterly miserable. My wife is terrible and impossible. Seeing you occasionally had been my one joy—my only consolation. And only to-night—before—you had been telling me not to come and see you any more. Now I feel our friendship is all over. I could not expect you to see me again. You are such an angel, that you will, if I ask you, I believe, try to wipe out from your memory this horrible evening! I would rather have died than it should have happened. Of course, you see now that by instinct Mary guessed right—I mean in knowing my feeling for you—though heaven knows I haven't deserved this. She's screaming for me, and I must stop. All I ask is, don't hate me! I'm so miserable when I think that you, beautiful angel as you are, might have belonged to me. I doubt if I shall be able to live this life much longer.

"In humblest apology, and with that deep feeling that writing can never express, your idolising

NIGEL.

"*P.S.*—I ought not to have written that. But I fear so much that I may not see you again, and that this may be my last letter, and I feel I would like you to know honestly all I feel for you. But words may not bear such burdens. Send me one word, only one word of pardon."

Bertha was obviously shocked and surprised at this letter. She folded it up, looking grave. Then she said to Madeline:

"What a very extraordinary thing it has been that both Mary and Percy have been suspicious and jealous of Nigel and myself, while there's been absolutely nothing in it!"

"But they both felt by instinct, perhaps, that that was no fault of his," returned Madeline.

"I have no sympathy with him," said Bertha, who seemed for her quite hard. "If he does like me, all the more he ought to have kept away. Besides, it's only because he wants to be amused! What right has he to make his wife unhappy, when he deliberately chose her, and to be willing—if he is willing—to smash up my happiness with Percy?"

"Of course that's horrid of him," said Madeline; "but somehow I do think his wife is rather awful; I think she might do anything. But won't you answer his letter?"

"Yes; I think I'd better write him a line," said Bertha.

She sat down and wrote:

"DEAR MR. HILLIER,—Pray don't think again of the unpleasant little incident.

"I have already forgotten it.

"I think that if you will make your children the interest of your life—though it's very impertinent of me to say so—happiness must come of it.

"Good-bye. Yours very sincerely,

"BERTHA KELLYNCH"

"I've written," said Bertha, "what I wouldn't mind either Percy or Mary seeing."

"I'm sure you have, dear. But Percy would rather you didn't write at all."

"Perhaps. But I think it's right. Besides, otherwise, he might write again, or even call."

"Yes, that's true."

CHAPTER XXIV

LADY KELLYNCH AT HOME

ALTHOUGH Lady Kellynch was a widow, and had had two sons (at the unusual interval of eighteen years), there was something curiously old-maidish about her—I should say that she had a set of qualities that were formerly known by that expression, as there are no such things nowadays as old maids and maiden aunts as contrasted to British matrons. There are merely married or unmarried women. And Lady Kellynch belonged to a long-forgotten type; she was no suffragette; politics did not touch her, and at fifty-four she did not regard herself as the modern middle-aged woman does. It never occurred to her for a moment, for example, to have lessons in the Tango or to learn ski-ing or any other winter sports, in a white jersey and cap. She was not seen clinging to the arm of a professor of roller-skating, nor did she go to fancy-dress balls as Folly or Romeo, as a Pierrette or Joan of Arc, as many of her contemporaries loved to do. She dressed magnificently and in the fashion of the day, and yet she always remained and looked extremely old-fashioned; and though she would wear her hats as they were made nowadays, her hair then had a look that did not go with it; no hairdresser or milliner could ever induce her to do it in a style later than 1887. The larger number of women have had some period of their lives when the fashion has happened to suit them, or when, for some reason or another, they have had a special success, and most of these cling fondly to that epoch. Lady Kellynch never got away from 1887 and the time of Queen Victoria's first Jubilee. All the fads of the hour seemed to have passed over her since then, from bicycling to flying, from classical dancing or ragtime to enthusiasm about votes for women; the various movements had passed over her without leaving any hurt or effect. Lady Kellynch had had a success in 1887; she cherished tenderly a photograph of herself in an enormous bustle, with an impossibly small waist, a thick high fringe over her eyes, and a tight dog-collar. The bald bare look about the ears, and the extraordinary figure resembling a switchback made her look very much older then than she did now. But more than one smart young soldier (now, probably, steady retired generals, who passed their time saying that the country was going to the dogs), an attaché long since married and sunk into domestic life, and one or two other men had greatly admired her; she had had her little dignified flirtations, much as she adored the late Sir Percy Kellynch; her portrait had been painted by Herkomer, and the Prince of Wales (as he then was) had looked at her through his opera glass during the performance of Gounod's *Romeo and Juliet*. These were things not to be forgotten. When her husband died, Percy married and Clifford went to school, and Lady Kellynch was left alone in her big house in South Kensington, she became again what I call old-maidish. She had a hundred little rules and fussy little arrangements, of which the slightest disorganisation drove her to distraction. She had long consultations every day with the cook at nine o'clock as to what was to be done with what was left. She liked to be domestic, and would stand over the man who was cleaning the windows and tell him how to do it. Certain things she liked to do herself.

In the drawing-room was a chandelier of the seventies, beautiful in its way, though out of date, and she used to take the lustres down and polish them with her own fingers, taking a great pride in doing this herself. She cared really for no one in the world but her two sons, but she was extremely fond, in her own way, of society and of receiving. She did not keep open house, and hers was not by any means casual hospitality. She hated anyone to call upon her unexpected and uninvited, except on the first and third Thursday of every month. She was very much surprised that in the rush of the present day people had a way of forgetting these days and calling on others. The first Thursday was peculiarly ill-treated and ignored, and preparations on that day were often wasted, while on the second Thursday she would come home and find a quantity of cards, belonging to more or less smart, if dull, people who had left them, with a sigh of relief at their mistake.

Lady Kellynch was good-natured in a cold kind of way, and even lavish; yet she had her queer, petty economies, and was always talking about a mysterious feat that she spoke of as *keeping the books down*, and was also fond of discovering tiny little dressmakers who used to be with some celebrated one and had now set up for themselves.

Lady Kellynch was very kind to these little dressmakers—she spoke of them as if they were minute to the point of being midgets or dwarfs

—she was really rather the curse of their lives, and after a while they would have been glad to dispense with her custom. She wanted them to do impossibilities, such as making her look exactly as she did at Queen Victoria's first Jubilee (the time when she was so much admired and had such a success), and yet making her look up-to-date now, without any of the horrid fast modern style.

When Clifford was at home things were considerably turned upside down, and when the time of his holidays drew to an end she was conscious of being relieved.

It was the first Thursday, and Lady Kellynch was at home. A day or two before Clifford had spent a day with Pickering and his mother. She had told him he might ask the boy to tea.

"Mother," said Clifford, who had received a note, "Pickering can't come to-day."

"Oh, indeed—what a pity."

She was really rather glad. Boys at an At Home were a bore and ate all the cake.

"Er—no—he can't come. But, I say, you won't mind, will you?—his mother's coming."

"His mother!" exclaimed Lady Kellynch, rather surprised.

"Er—yes—I asked her. I thought, perhaps, you wouldn't mind. She wants to know you."

"Really? It's very kind of her, I'm sure."

"You see, in a way, though she's awfully rich—I suppose she's a bit of a—you know what I mean—a sort of a *nouveau riche*. She wants to visit a few decent people, especially not too young."

"Oh, indeed!"

"She says it'll sort of pose her, and help her to get into society."

"What curious things to say to a boy."

"Oh, she's awfully jolly, mother. She says everything that comes into her head. She's ripping—I do like her."

"Who was she?" asked his mother, with a rather chilling accent.

"I'm sure I don't know who she was," said the boy. "I can tell you who she is: she's the prettiest woman I've ever seen."

"Good gracious me!"

"We had awful larks," went on Clifford. "She played with us and Pickering's kiddy sister. We danced the Tango and had charades. You can't think what fun it was. And we had tableaux. Mrs. Pickering and I did a lovely tableau, 'Death in the Desert.' She fell down dead suddenly, on the sand, you know, and I was a vulture. I'm an awfully good vulture. And I vultured about and hopped round her for some considerable time."

"Horrible!" cried Lady Kellynch. "Revolting! What an unpleasant subject for a game."

"It wasn't a game: it was a proper tableau: we had a curtain and all that sort of thing. They said I made a capital vulture. I pecked at Mrs. Pickering. It was a great success."

"Dear me! Was it indeed? Well, if this lady's coming, you'd better go and wash your hands," said Lady Kellynch, who felt a disposition to snub Clifford on the subject.

"Of course I will! I say, mother, what cakes have you got?"

"Really, Clifford, I think you can leave that to me."

"They have jolly little *foie gras* sandwiches at the Pickerings."

"I daresay they have."

"Can I go and tell cook to make some?"

"Most certainly not, Clifford!" cried the indignant mother.

"But if there aren't any, she might miss them," said Clifford.

"She will probably enjoy the change."

"You can't think how pretty she is! I say, mother."

"Yes, dear."

"I say, can't you have fur put round the edge of your shoes!"

"Fur round the edge of my shoes!" she repeated in a hollow voice.

He twisted his hands together self-consciously.

"Mrs. Pickering had an awful ripping violet sort of dress, and violet satin boots with fur round the edge. . . . I noticed them when we played 'Death in the Desert.' I thought they were rather pretty."

"Extremely bad style, I should think. At any rate, not the sort of thing that I should dream of wearing. Now get along."

Clifford went down to the kitchen and worried the cook with descriptions of the gorgeous cakes he had seen at the Pickerings till she said that his ma had better accept her notice, and engage the Pickerings' cook instead.

"Orders from you, Master Clifford, I will not take. And now you've got it straight. *For grars* in the afternoon is a thing I don't hold with and never would hold with, and I've lived in the best families. There's some nice sandwiches made of *gentlemen's relish* made of Blootes' paste, your ma's always 'ad since I've been here; it's done for her and the best families I've lived in. *Fors grars* is served at the end of dinner with apsia and jelly, or else in one of them things with crust on the top and truffles. But for tea I consider it quite out of place."

She went on to say that if she couldn't have her kitchen to herself without the young gentlemen of the house putting their oar in, she would leave that day month.

Clifford fled, frightened, and tidied himself.

At about five, when two or three old cronies of Lady Kellynch's were sitting round, talking about the royal family, a gigantic motor, painted white, came to the door, and Mrs. Pickering was announced.

She was very young and very pretty. Her hair was the very brightest gold, and she had rather too much mauve and too much smile; she almost curtsied to her hostess, and instantly gave that lady the impression that she must have been not so very long ago the principal boy at some popular pantomine.

CHAPTER XXV

MRS. PICKERING

"OUR boys are such very great friends—I really felt I must know you!" cried Mrs. Pickering in the most cordial way. She spoke with a very slight Cockney accent. She bristled with aigrettes and sparkled with jewels. Her bodice was cut very low, her sleeves very short, and her white gloves came over the braceleted elbows. She wore a very high, narrow turban, green satin shoes and stockings, and altogether was dressed rather excessively; she looked like one of Louis Bauer's drawings in *Punch*. She was certainly most striking in appearance, and a little alarming in a quiet room, but most decidedly pretty and with a very pleasant smile.

Lady Kellynch received her with great courtesy, but was not sufficiently adaptable and subtle to conceal at once the fact that Mrs. Pickering's general appearance and manner had completely taken her breath away. Also, she was annoyed that Lady Gertrude Münster was there to-day. Lady Gertrude was one of her great cards. She was a clever, glib, battered-looking, elderly woman, who, since her husband had once been at the Embassy in Vienna, had assumed a slight foreign accent; it was meant to be Austrian but sounded Scotch. Lady Gertrude looked rather muffled and seemed to have more thick veils and feather boas on than was necessary for the time of the year. She was an old friend of Lady Kellynch's, and they detested each other, but never missed an opportunity of meeting, chiefly in order to impress each other, in one way or another, or cause each other envy or annoyance.

Lady Kellynch was always very specially careful whom she asked, or allowed, to meet Lady Gertrude. She had wanted Bertha particularly to-day and was vexed at this unexpected arrival.

"Your daughter-in-law, my dear?" asked Lady Gertrude, in a surprised tone, putting up her long tortoiseshell glass.

"Oh *dear*, no, Gertrude! Surely you know Bertha by sight! I never had the pleasure of meeting Mrs. Pickering before."

"Charmed to meet you," said Mrs. Pickering again, giving a kind of curtsy and smiling at Lady Gertrude. "Ah, there's my little friend!

Well, Cliff, didn't we have fun the other day? Eustace was sorry he couldn't come to-day. We had the greatest larks, Lady Kellynch! I play with the kids just like one of themselves. We've got a great big room fixed up on purpose for Cissie and Eustace to romp. We haven't been there very long yet, Lady Kellynch. You know that big corner house in Hamilton Place leading into Park Lane. My husband thinks there's nothing good enough for the children. If it comes to that, he thinks there's nothing good enough for me." She giggled. "He gave me this emerald brooch only this morning. 'Oh, Tom,' I said, 'what a silly you are. You don't want to make a fuss about birthdays now we're getting on.' But he is silly about me! It's a nice little thing, isn't it?" she said, showing it to Lady Gertrude, who put up her glass to examine it.

"Lady Gertrude Münster—Mrs. Pickering," said Lady Kellynch. "Some tea?"

"Thanks, no tea. It's a pretty little thing, isn't it, Lady Münster?"

"Rather nice. Are they real?" asked Lady Gertrude.

Mrs. Pickering laughed very loudly. "You're getting at me. I shouldn't be so pleased with it if it came out of a cracker! But what I always say about presents, Lady Kellynch, is, it isn't so much the kind thought, it's the value of the gift I look at. No, I meant——"

"What you said, I suppose," said Lady Gertrude, who was rather enjoying herself, as she saw her hostess was irritated.

"Whoever's that pretty picture over there?"

Mrs. Pickering got up and went to look at the piano.

Lady Kellynch still retained (with several other *passé* fashions) the very South Kensington custom of covering up her large piano with a handsome piece of Japanese embroidery, which was caught up at intervals into bunchy bits of drapery, fastened by pots of flowers with sashes round their necks and with a very large number of dark photographs in frames, so very artistic in their heavy shading that one saw only a gleam of light occasionally on the tip of the nose or the back of the neck—all the rest in shadow—all with very large dashing signatures slanting across the corners, chiefly of former dim social celebrities or present well-known obscurities. The photograph she was looking at now was a pretty one of Bertha.

"Ah, that is my daughter-in-law."

Lady Kellynch pointed it out to Lady Gertrude.

"This *is* pretty—what you can see of it."

"Here she is herself."

Bertha came in.

"Mrs. Pickering—Mrs. Percy Kellynch."

The hostess gave Bertha an imploring look. She took in the situation at a glance and drew Mrs. Pickering a little aside, where Lady Gertrude could not listen to her piercing Cockney accent.

Clifford joined the group.

If Lady Kellynch had been, almost against her will, reminded by something in her visitor of a pantomime, Bertha saw far more. She was convinced at once that the rich eldest son of Pickering, the Jam King, had been dazzled and carried away, some fourteen years ago, and bestowed his enormous fortune and himself, probably against his family's wish, on a little provincial chorus girl. Her cheery determination to get on, and an evident sense of humour, made Bertha like her, in spite of her snobbishness and her manner. She was a change, at least, to meet here, and when Mrs. Pickering produced her card, which she did to everyone to whom she spoke, Bertha promised to call and asked her also. Of course one would have to be a shade careful whom one asked to meet her, but probably it would be a jolly house to go to. And nowadays! Still, Bertha was a little surprised that Clifford was so infatuated with the mother of his friend. She forgot that at twelve years old one is not fastidious; the taste is crude. If he admired Bertha's fair hair, he thought Mrs. Pickering's brilliant gold curls still prettier. Besides, Mrs. Pickering petted and made much of him, and was very kind.

She stayed much too long for a first visit, and as she went of course produced another card, saying to the muffled lady:

"Pleased to have met you, Lady Münster. I hope you'll call and see our new house. We're going to give a ball soon. We're entertaining this season."

"She certainly is," murmured Lady Gertrude. Then, as she left: "My dear, where do you pick up your extraordinary friends?"

This was a particularly nasty one for Lady Kellynch, who made such a point of her exclusiveness.

"Clifford is responsible for this, I think," said Bertha. "The boys are at the same school, and they've been very kind to him. I think she's very amusing, and a good sort."

"Oh, quite a character! She told me she met her husband at Blackpool. He fell in love with her when she was playing Prince Charming in No. 2 B Company on tour with the pantomime *Little Miss Muffet*."

"Just what one would have thought!" said Lady Kellynch, rather tragically.

"I've come to ask you if you'll go with Percy to the Queen's Hall to-morrow," Bertha said. "He wants you to come so much."

The mother delightedly consented.

"Curious fad that is the mania for serious music," said Lady Gertrude. "You don't share your husband's taste for it, it seems?"

"Well, I do, really. But it's such a treat for him to take his mother out!" said Bertha tactfully.

"I say, Bertha, may I come back with you? I'm going back to school next week."

"Of course you shall, if your mother likes."

His mother was glad to agree. She did not feel inclined to discuss Mrs. Pickering with the boy that evening.

"Try and make him see what an awful woman she is," she murmured.

"I will; but it isn't dangerous," laughed Bertha. "Madeline is spending the evening with me to-morrow."

"Oh yes, that nice quiet girl. By the way, do you know, I heard she was engaged to young Charles Hillier. And then somewhere else I was told it was Mr. Rupert Denison."

"It's neither," calmly replied Bertha, "But I believe each of them proposed to her."

"Is that a fact? Dear me! Just fancy her refusing them both! What a grief for poor Mrs. Irwin!"

Bertha laughed as she remembered that as a matter of fact Madeline had accepted both, within two days.

CHAPTER XXVI

NEWS FROM VENICE

MADELINE was sitting one afternoon with her mother in their little Chippendale flat, all .inlaid mahogany and old-fashioned chintz, china in cabinets, and miniatures on crimson velvet; it was so perfectly in keeping that the very parlourmaid's cap looked Chippendale, and it somehow suggested Hugh Thomson's illustrations to Jane Austen's books. Mrs. Irwin and Madeline were not, however, in the least degree like Miss Austen's heroines and their mothers, except that Mrs. Irwin, though very thin and elegant, had this one resemblance to the immortal Mrs. Bennet in "Pride and Prejudice": "the serious object of her life was to get her daughter married; its solace, gossiping and news." Also she had much of the same querulousness, and complained every night of nerves, and each morning of insomnia.

Madeline was reading John Addington Symonds' Renaissance and everything that she could get on the subject of Italian history and cinquecento art. These studies she pursued still as a sort of monument to Rupert, or as a link with him. And to-day, as she was waiting for Bertha to call and take her out, she received a letter from him, from Venice.

It was one of his long, friendly, cultured letters; making no allusion to any thoughts of becoming more than friends to each other, and no reference to the interlude of his proposal, or the episode of her engagement to Charlie. This memory seemed to have faded away, and he wrote in his old instructive way a long letter in his pretty little handwriting, speaking of gondoliers, Savonarola, hotels, pictures, lagoons, fashions and the weather. This last, he declared to be so unbearable that he thought of coming back to London before very long. He asked for an answer to his letter, and wished to know what she was reading, what concerts she had been to, and whether she had seen the exhibition at the Goupil Gallery.

But though it took her back to long before the period of his love-letter, and he appeared to wish the whole affair to be forgotten, it gave her considerable satisfaction. He wanted to hear of her, and, what was more, he was coming back. Of course Mrs. Irwin saw that the letter was from him, and she remarked that she had always said everyone had a right to their own letters, and that after twenty-one, nowadays, she supposed girls could do exactly what they liked, which she thought was only fair; that mothers, very rightly, hardly counted in the present day, were regarded as nobody, and were treated with no confidence of any kind, of which she thoroughly approved; that Madeline's new coat and skirt suited her very badly and did not fit; and that grey had never been her colour.

Madeline's reply to this was to place the long letter into her mother's hand.

Having read it, Mrs. Irwin said she did not wish to force anybody's confidence, and she was evidently disappointed at its contents. However, she advised her daughter to answer without loss of time.

The conversation was interrupted by Bertha's arrival.

"You know my brother-in-law, Clifford?" she said. "The funny boy has 'littery' tastes and began writing an historical play! But he got tired of it and now he's taken to writing verses. I've brought you one of his poems; they're so funny I thought it would amuse you. Fancy if a brother of Percy's should grow up to be a 'littery gent'. I suspect it to be addressed to the mother of his beloved friend, Pickering. He is devoted to her."

"Where are you going to-day?" inquired Mrs. Irwin.

"I'm taking Madeline to see Miss Belvoir. She has rather amusing afternoons. Her brother, Fred Belvoir, whom she lives with, is a curious sort of celebrity. When he went down from Oxford they had a sort of funeral procession because he was so popular. He's known on every race-course; he's a great hunting man, an authority on musical comedy, and is literary too—he writes for *Town Topics*. Miss Belvoir is the most good-natured woman in the world, and so intensely hospitable that she asks everyone to lunch or dinner the first time she meets them, and sometimes without having been introduced, and she asks everyone to bring their friends. They have a charming flat on the Thames Embankment and a dear little country house called The Lurch, where her brother often leaves her. They're mad on private theatricals, too, and are always dressing up."

"It sounds rather fun," said Madeline.

"Not very exclusive," suggested her mother.

"No, not a bit. But it's great fun," said Bertha, "and I've heard people say that you can be as exclusive as you like at Miss Belvoir's by bringing your own set and talking only to them. People who go to her large parties often don't know her by sight; she's so lost in the crowd, and she never remembers anybody, or knows them again. To be ever so little artistic is a sufficient passport to be asked to the Belvoirs'. In fact if a brother-in-law of a friend of yours once sent an article to a magazine which was not inserted, or if your second cousin once met Tree at a party, and was not introduced to him, that is quite sufficient to make you a welcome guest there. Now that my little brother-in-law has written a poem, I shall have a *raison d'être* in being there. You'll see, Madeline, you'll enjoy yourself."

CHAPTER XXVII

ANOTHER ANONYMOUS LETTER

"OH, Bertha, I've heard from Rupert again," said Madeline, as they drove along.

"I saw you'd had a letter from that talented young cul-de-sac," replied Bertha.

"What do you mean?"

"Nothing. I didn't mean anything. I like to tease you, and you must confess that he's the sort of man—well, nothing ever seems to get much forrarder with him! What does he say?"

"It's just the sort of letter he wrote long before he ever dreamt of proposing to me."

"Well, I think that's rather a good sign. He's reassumed his early manner. I believe he's going to work his way up all over again—all through the beaten paths, and ignore the incident that hurt his vanity, and then propose again. We may have rather fun here to-day. Sometimes there are only a few fly-blown celebrities, and sometimes there are very new beginners without a future, debutantes who will never *débuter*, singers who can't sing, actors who never have any engagements, and editors who are just thinking of bringing out a paper. Miss Belvoir collects people who are unknown but prominent, noticeable and yet obscure. Here we are."

While Bertha and Madeline were being entertained in Miss Belvoir's drawing-room something more serious was happening to Percy.

The day after the Hilliers' party Nigel had a terrible quarrel with his wife, and he threatened that if she ever again lost her self-control and disgraced him or herself by anything in the way of a scene, that he would leave her and never come back. This really frightened her, for she knew she had behaved unpardonably. She would not have minded so very much if he had gone away for a little while, but how was she to prevent the Kellynches going to the same place—even travelling with him? She had been amazed to see Bertha. At the time she sent the letters there had certainly been a marked change, a new movement, as she thought. They had had an effect, without a doubt, though how or what she hardly knew, but she supposed she had roused Percy's suspicions and he had stopped the meetings. And then Mrs. Kellynch calmly came to the party without her husband, which seemed to prove she knew nothing of the letters, and disappeared at once with Nigel into the shaded conversation-room, snatching her host and openly flirting with him in the most marked way! It had been too much for her self-restraint. But now Mary saw she had gone too far. Her open fury had been less successful than her secret intriguing, so she apologised most humbly, entreated him to forgive her, and even swore never to interfere again. He was to be quite free. He might see Mrs. Kellynch whenever he liked. But all this was, of course, too late for Nigel, since Bertha herself had declined to see him again, and Mary resolved to start afresh. Probably the husband had lost his suspicions and they must be roused again. If only Bertha had told him all that had happened at the party, and if only Percy had frankly shown her the letters and concealed nothing from her, there would have been no more trouble. But each of them, from mistaken reasons, had concealed these facts from the other. So, within a week of the entertainment, when he had been so enchanted with her coming home early, Percy received another shock, another warning anonymous letter.

It told him that his wife had made herself so conspicuous with Nigel Hillier that the hostess had requested her to leave, also that their meetings and their intrigue were the talk of London. He was again advised to put a stop to it, but was not this time given any day and hour or place to find them.

This time Percy said nothing to his wife. He made up his mind to have it out, for several reasons, with Nigel. Though he was angry and jealous, he now did not believe for a moment that Bertha was in any way to blame, but simply that Nigel must be paying her marked attention, and whatever the cause of the talk he was determined to stop it.

He thought for some time about where he could have an interview with Nigel. He could not ask him to his own house, nor could he go and see him at Grosvenor Street. His former idea of talking at the club he saw to be impossible.

He sat down and wrote:

"DEAR HILLIER,—I want to have a talk with you. Will you come and see me at my chambers at four o'clock the day after to-morrow? No. 7 Essex Court, Temple. Yours sincerely,

"PERCIVAL KELLYNCH."

Nigel was amazed to receive this, and rather alarmed too. It was about a week since he had had Bertha's little letter, but he had made no attempt to see her since.

He answered immediately that he would call at the time appointed and passed a very restless day and night beforehand.

CHAPTER XXVIII

AN INTERVIEW

NIGEL, filled with curiosity, and rather anxious, arrived punctually to the moment. He was shown into Percy's chambers by a stout and prosperous-looking middle-aged clerk, with a gold watch-chain.

He waited there for some minutes, walking slowly up and down the room and examining it. It was a very dull, serious room, almost depressing. On the large table lay bulbous important-looking briefs, tied up with red tape. Framed caricatures of judges and eminent barristers from *Vanity Fair* hung round the walls. The furniture was scarce, large and heavy. On the mantelpiece was a framed photograph with a closed leather cover. It looked interesting and expensive, and Nigel with his quick movements had the curiosity to go across the room to open it. It contained two lovely photographs of Bertha: one in furs and a hat, the other in evening dress. It irritated

Nigel. . . . A sound of footsteps gave him only just time to close it with a spring, and sit down.

Percy came in looking as Nigel had never seen him look before. There had been an unimportant case in court, but he had been unable to get away before. He was so orderly as a rule that he detested keeping anybody waiting. He looked flushed and hurried, and his black smooth hair was extraordinarily rough and wild. Of course, Nigel remembered, he had just taken off his wig. There was a red line on his forehead, the mark left by this ornament. The effect made him look like a different person. He threw off his coat and spoke seriously and rather formally.

"Sorry, Hillier. Delayed in court. Hope I haven't kept you?"

"It doesn't matter in the least," Nigel answered in his cheery way.

Nigel was looking exceedingly at ease, and happy, though the manner was really assumed to-day. He was very smartly dressed, with light gloves and a buttonhole of violets, and looked a gay contrast to Percy, with his unusually rough hair and solemn expression.

"I was very interested. I don't think I've ever seen a barrister's chambers before. Jolly rooms you've got here. What a charming place the Temple is. . . . Well! I've been simply dying of curiosity," he went on, with a pleasant smile.

"Sit down," said Percy. "Have a cigarette?"

Nigel lighted up. Percy did not.

"It's not very pleasant what I want to say to you. It's simply that I don't want you to come to our house any more."

Nigel looked surprised and coloured slightly.

"And may I ask your reason?"

"I don't see why I should give it, but I will. I don't wish you to see my wife any more."

"This is very extraordinary, Kellynch! Why?"

"I've reason to believe that your old friendship has been the cause of some talk—some scandal. I don't like it. I won't have it, and that's sufficient. I insist on you avoiding her in future."

Nigel stared blankly.

"I can only agree of course. I'll do just as you tell me. But I think, as we've known each other so long, that it would be only fair for you to tell me what is your reason for thinking this."

Nigel walked up and down the room, turned suddenly and said: "What has put this idea into your head?"

Percy hesitated a moment.

"I'll tell you if you like. But, mind, I want no explanations. I needn't say," he glanced at the closed photograph, "that I could have no doubt of any kind. . . . But I have a right to choose my friends and my wife's also."

"She doesn't object?"

Percy frowned and looked him straight in the face.

"I undertake to say she will not object. We'll make this conversation as short as we can. You've asked me my reason and I'll give it you. I've had a series of extraordinary anonymous letters concerning you."

Nigel stared, horrified.

"She knows nothing about it," continued Percy, "and I attach no importance to them, except, as I say, they show that your acquaintance must have been misconstrued, and I won't have a shadow . . . on her."

"This is rather hard on me, Kellynch. However, I have the satisfaction of knowing my conscience is absolutely clear, and of course, I'll do just as you wish. Have you any objection to showing me the letters?"

After a moment's pause, Percy said:

"No. I don't know that I have. I've got them here. I meant to shove them in the fire, but I'll let you read them first, if you like."

He went to a drawer, unlocked it, gave Nigel the letters, and watched him while he read them.

The moment Nigel glanced at them he knew they were written by Mary. He remembered by the dates when she had had the typewriter; he remembered, even, seeing some of the white notepaper. He read them all. Then he looked up and said:

"Kellynch, it's good of you to show these to me. I'm sorry to say I know who wrote them. The earlier ones telling of the appointments are all perfectly true, but entirely misrepresented. They can all be explained."

"I understand that," said Percy. "Of course the suggestion and the impression the writer tries to give are absolutely false."

"Quite so. May I burn the letters now?"

There was a fire and Nigel threw them into it. He saw no point in keeping them to confront Mary with. She would confess anyhow.

"May I ask one thing more?"

"My wife knows nothing about them," repeated Percy.

Nigel thought what a pity that was. If she had, she would not have come to the party; things might have been tided over. But now. . . . He had no hope of the wish of his life, he was as furious as a spoilt child who is deprived of a favourite toy—or, rather, disappointed of all hopes of getting one. He became more and more angry with Percy and longed to annoy him. The fellow was too satisfied—too lucky—he had everything too much his own way!

"May I ask one thing?" said Nigel, as the letters were burning and he gave them one last irritated touch with the poker, "may I ask, does this affair give you the impression that I—only I naturally—had any—er—motives in trying to see Mrs. Kellynch often? If I may put it plainly, did you think I cared for her in a way that I had no right to?"

"To tell you the honest truth," said Percy, "as I choose to be frank with you, I won't say you had . . . motives, but I have the impression that you—er—admire her too much."

Nigel waited a moment.

"And there you are perfectly right, Kellynch."

Percy started up, looking a little pale.

Nigel had got a little of his revenge.

He had annoyed the comfortable Percy.

"But let me say that all this time I have never, never shown it by word or look. Our talks were almost entirely about Madeline Irwin and my brother, or about Rupert Denison. Your wife is so exceedingly kind and good that she wished to see Miss Madeline as happy as herself."

"Yes, yes, I know all that," said Percy impatiently.

"I shall follow your wishes to the very letter," said Nigel. "You see how very open I've been. How will you explain to her that I drop your acquaintance?"

"I think I shall tell her now," said Percy, "that I had received a letter and that I've seen you. But I shall tell her we parted the best of friends, and nothing must be done, above all things, to annoy or agitate her."

He looked at the closed leather case again.

"Just now I want to take special care of her. I daresay she won't notice not meeting you, as we're not going out in the evening the rest of the season nor entertaining."

Nigel looked amazed. An idea occured to him that caused him absurd mortification. It dawned upon his mind that perhaps Bertha was going to have her wish. If so, he would be forgotten more completely than ever.

"Forgive me for asking, Kellynch. I think you've been very good to me, really. I trust your wife is not ill?"

"Ill?—oh dear, no."

Percy smiled a smile that to Nigel seemed maddeningly complacent. "She merely wants a little care for a time. We shall go to the country very early this year. As a matter of fact, it's something she's very pleased about." He stopped.

Nigel gave a pale smile. Percy was too irritating!

"Well, you were right not to worry her about the letters. I'm very sorry for the whole thing. I think it's been hard on me, Kellynch."

He stood up.

"Good-bye, Hillier!"

Nigel held out his hand; Percy shook it coldly.

As he went to the door, taking up his hat and stick, Nigel said:

"I sincerely hope you won't miss me!"

CHAPTER XXIX

NIGEL AND MARY

NIGEL rushed back. On his way, he decided that he had got a real excuse for a holiday; he had every right to go away for a time from such a wife; and he found himself thinking chiefly about where he would go and how he would amuse himself. If the husband had only known it, Bertha had already, if not exactly forbidden him the house, discouraged his calling, almost as distinctly, though more kindly, than Percy did. Still, if Percy had not given him that piece of information, he would have remained in London, and left it to chance that they might meet again somehow. He was such an optimist, and was really so very much in love with her. Curious that this news of Bertha should annoy and should excite him so much! Why, it seemed to him to be a matter of more importance and far more interest than in his own wife's case. That he had taken quite as a matter of course, an ordinary everyday occurrence "which would give her something to do." He was really disappointed when he found that Mary did not absorb herself in her children, and found she was only anxious—foolishly anxious—that he should not think that they could take his place as companions.

Nigel was affectionate by nature, and if Mary had insisted on that note—if she had made him proud of his children, encouraged his affection for them, if she had played the madonna—his affection for her would have been immensely increased. She would have had a niche in his heart—a respect and tenderness, even if she had never been able to make him entirely faithful, which, perhaps, only one woman could have done. But, instead of that, Mary had been jealous and silly and violently exacting. She wished him to be her slave and under her thumb, and yet she wanted him to be her lover. Every word she had ever spoken, everything she had ever done since their marriage had had the exact contrary effect of what she desired. She had sent him further and further away from her. That she knew he had married her for her money embittered her and yet made her tyrannical. She wanted to take advantage of that fact, in a way that no man could endure. Yet she was to be pitied. Anyone so exacting must be terribly unhappy.

It was not in Nigel, either, to care long for anyone who cared for him so much. And even if Bertha, who was now his ideal and his dream, had been as devoted to him as Mary, and shown it in anything like the same sort of way, he would in time have become cool and ceased to appreciate her. He thought now that he would always adore her, and yet, when they had been actually engaged, it had been he who had allowed it to lapse. He might think that he cared for her far more now and understood her better, and now no worldly object would induce him to give up the possibility of their passing their lives together. And yet the fact remained. She had loved him as a girl—worshipped him. But he had broken it off. So now that he has lost all hope of his wish, he does not, strictly speaking, deserve any sympathy; yet all emotional suffering appeals to one's pity rather than to one's sense of justice. And Nigel was miserable.

The letter Bertha had sent him the other day, though it put an end to their meeting, had a sort of fragrance; a tender kindness about it. He could make himself believe that she also was a little sorry. Perhaps she did it more from motives of duty than from her own wish; something about it left a little glamour, and he had still hope that somehow or other circumstances might alter so much that even so they might be friends again. But now! it was very different. Percy's quiet satisfaction showed that they were on the most perfect terms, and he could imagine Bertha's delight—her high spirits—and her charming little ways of showing her pleasure. It forced itself on his mind against his will, that she was very much in love with Percy after all these ten years, difficult as it seemed to him to realise it.

So they were hardly going out any more! So they were going to the country early to have a sort of second honeymoon! It seemed to him that after ten years of gay camaraderie they were now suddenly going to behave like lovers, like a newly married young couple.

How sickening it was, and how absorbed she would be now! People always made much more of an event like that when it happened after some years. Personally he tried to think it made him like her less, at any rate it seemed to make her far more removed from him. But all the real estrangement had been caused undoubtedly by his wife.

On the whole, to be just, that pompous ass, as he called him, Percy Kellynch, had really behaved very well. He had accused Nigel of nothing; he had suggested nothing about his wife, who was still, evidently, on a pedestal; he had really done the right thing and been considerate to her in the highest degree. Any man who cared for his wife would have naturally requested him, Nigel, to keep away. And it was really decent, frightfully decent of him, to let him see the letters, really kind and fair. Of course what put old Percy in a good temper, in spite of all, was this news, and, no doubt, Bertha was being angelic to him.

Nigel made up his mind to try and throw it off. But he couldn't do it by staying with his wife.

To look at her would be agonising now.

Still he made up his mind he would be calm, he would not be unkind to her; he would be firm, and, as far as possible, have no sort of scene.

When he went in, she was sitting in the boudoir looking out of the window as usual. She saw him before he came in. It was not six o'clock yet and quite light.

"Well, Nigel darling?" She ran up to him.

He moved away.

"Please don't, Mary. I've got something serious to speak to you about."

She turned pale, guiltily.

"What is it? What on earth is it?"

"You shall hear. Shall we talk about it now, or wait till after dinner? I think I'd rather wait. I've got a bit of a headache."

"After dinner, then," murmured Mary.

This was very unlike her. Had she had nothing on her conscience, nothing she was afraid of, she would never have ceased questioning and worrying him to get it all out of him.

He went up to his room, and asked her to leave him, and this she actually did. She wanted time to think!

With the weak good nature that was in Nigel, curiously side by side with a certain cruel hardness, he now felt a little sorry for her. It must be awful to be waiting like this. And she really had been in the wrong. It was an appalling thing to do—mad, hysterical, dangerous. It might have caused far more trouble than it had! Suppose Percy had believed it all!

Nigel thought of scandals, divorces, all sorts of things. Yes, after all, Kellynch had really been kind; and clever. He was not a bad sort. Then Nigel found that last little letter of Bertha's. How sweet it was! But he saw through it now, that she was deeply happy and didn't want to be bothered with him. She forgave the scene his wife had made at the party, as not one woman in a hundred would do—but she didn't want him. The moment she realised that he wanted to flirt with her, that there was even a chance of his loving her, she was simply bored. Yes, that was it—gay, amusing, witty, attractive Nigel bored her! Dull, serious, conventional Percy did not! She was in love with him.

In books and plays it was always the other way: it was the husband that was the bore; but romances and comedies are often far away from life. Curious as it seemed, this was life, and Nigel realised it. He destroyed her letter and went down to dinner.

They were quiet at dinner, talked a little only for the servants. Nigel asked about the little girl.

"How's Marjorie getting on with her music lessons?"

Mary answered in a low voice that the teacher thought she had talent. . . .

They were left alone.

"Well, what is it, Nigel?" She spoke in querulous, frightened voice.

They were sitting in the boudoir again. Coffee had been left on the table.

Nigel lighted a cigarette.

He was still a little sorry for her. Then he said:

"Look here, Mary, I'm sorry to say I've found out you've been doing a very terrible thing! I ask you not to deny it, because I know it. The only chance of our ever being in peace together again, or in peace at all, is for you to speak the truth."

She did not answer.

"I've forgiven heaps of things—frightful tempers, mad suspicions, that disgraceful scene you made at our party—but I always thought you were honourable and truthful. What you've done is very dishonourable. Don't make it worse by denying it." He paused. "You have written five anonymous letters, dictated in typewriting, about me and Mrs. Kellynch to her husband. I don't know what you thought, but you certainly tried to give the impression that our harmless conversations meant something more. That there was an intrigue going on. Did you really think this, may I ask?"

"Yes, I did," she said, in a low voice, looking down.

"Well, first allow me to assure you that you are entirely wrong. It was completely false. Can't you see now how terrible it was to suggest these absolute lies as facts to her husband? Did you write the letters?"

"Yes, I did; I was in despair. I couldn't think of anything else to stop it."

Nigel gave a sigh of relief.

"Thank God you've admitted it, Mary. I'm glad of that. At least if we have the truth between us, we know where we are."

"Did she—did she—tell you?"

"She knows nothing whatever about it," said Nigel. "She has never been told, and never will be. You need worry no more about the letters. Her husband gave them to me this afternoon, and I destroyed them before him. And he doesn't know who wrote them."

Nigel forgot that he had told Percy or did not choose to say.

"They're completely wiped out, and will be forgotten by the person to whom you sent them. The whole affair is cleared up and finished and regarded as an unfortunate act of folly."

"Oh, Nigel!" Mary burst into tears. "You're very good."

"Now listen, Mary. . . . I can't endure to stay with you any more at present."

"What!" she screamed.

"If I continue this existence with you I shall grow to hate it. I wish to go away for a time."

"You want to leave me!"

"Unless I go now for a time to try and get over this act of yours, I tell you frankly that I shall leave you altogether."

He spoke sternly.

"If you will have the decency not to oppose my wishes, I will go away for six or seven weeks, and when I come back we'll try and take up our life again a little differently. You must be less jealous and exacting and learn to control yourself. I will then try to forget and we'll try to get on better together. But I must go. My nerves won't stand it any longer."

She sobbed, leaning her head on the back of an arm-chair.

"If you agree to this without the slightest objection," said Nigel, "I will come and join you and the children somewhere in the first week in August. Till then I'm going abroad, but I don't exactly know where. You shall have my address, and, of course, I shall write. I may possibly go to Venice. I have a friend there."

She still said nothing, but cried bitterly. She was in despair at the idea of his leaving her, but secretly felt she might have been let off less lightly.

One thing Nigel resolved. He would not let her know he had been forbidden the house. She would be too pleased at having succeeded. But he said:

"One thing you may as well know, I shall see nothing more of the Kellynches, because they are going into the country in a few days. They have had no quarrel, they are perfectly devoted to each other, and she has not the faintest idea of it. So you see you haven't done the harm, or caused the pain you tried to, except to me. I was ashamed when I saw——"

"Oh, Nigel, forgive me! I am sorry! Don't go away!"

"Unless I go away now, I shall go altogether. Don't cry. Try to cheer up!"

With these words he left the room.

CHAPTER XXX

MISS BELVOIR

WE left Bertha and Madeline in the lift going up to call on Miss Belvoir. This lady was sitting by the fire, holding a screen. She came forward and greeted them with great cordiality. She was a small, dark, amiable-looking woman about thirty. Her hair and eyes were of a blackness one rarely sees, her complexion was clear and bright, her figure extremely small and trim. Without being exactly pretty, she was very agreeable to the eye, and also had the attraction of looking remarkably different from other people. Indeed her costume was so uncommon as to be on the verge of eccentricity. Her face had a slightly Japanese look, and she increased this effect by wearing a gown of which a part was decidedly Japanese. In fact it was a kimono covered with embroidery in designs consisting of a flight of storks, some chrysanthemums, and a few butterflies, in the richest shades of blue. In the left-hand corner were two little yellow men fighting with a sword in each hand; otherwise it was all blue. It was almost impossible to keep one's eyes from this yellow duel; the little embroidered figures looked so fierce and emotional and appeared to be enjoying themselves so much.

The room in which Miss Belvoir received her friends was very large, long and low, and had a delightful view of the river from the Embankment. It was a greyish afternoon, vague and misty, and one saw from the windows views that looked exactly like pictures by Whistler. The room was furnished in a Post-Impressionist style, chiefly in red, black and brown; the colours were all plain—that is to say, there were no designs except on the ceiling, which was cosily covered with large, brilliantly tinted, life-sized parrots.

Miss Belvoir's brother, Fred, often declared that when he came home late, which he generally did—between six and nine in the morning were his usual hours—he always had to stop himself from getting a gun, and he was afraid that some day he might lose his self-control and be tempted to shoot the parrots. He was an excellent shot.

The room was full of low bookcases crammed with books, and large fat cushions on the floor. They looked extremely comfortable, but as a matter of fact nobody ever liked sitting on them. When English people once overcame their natural shyness so far as to sit down on them, they were afraid they would never be able to get up again.

Three or four people were dotted about the room, but no one had ventured on the cushions. There was one young lady whose hair was done in the early Victorian style, parted in the middle, with bunches of curls each side. As far as her throat she appeared to be strictly a Victorian—very English, about 1850—but from that point she suddenly became Oriental, and for the rest was dressed principally in what looked like beaded curtains.

Leaning on the mantelpiece and smoking a cigarette with great ease of manner was a striking and agreeable-looking young man, about eight and twenty, whom Miss Belvoir introduced as Mr. Bevan Fairfield. He was fair and good-looking, very dandified in dress, and with a rather humorously turned-up nose and an excessively fluent way of speaking.

"I was just scolding Miss Belvoir," he said, "when you came in. She's been playing me the trick she's always playing. She gets me here under the pretext that some celebrity's coming and then they don't turn up. Signor Semolini, the Futurist, I was asked to meet. And then she gets a telegram—or says she does—that he can't come. Very odd, very curious, they never can come—at any rate when I'm here. Some people would rather say, 'Fancy, I was asked to Miss Belvoir's the other day to meet Semolini, only he didn't turn up,' than not say anything at all. Some people think it's a distinction not to have met Semolini at Miss Belvoir's."

"It's quite a satisfactory distinction," remarked Bertha. "Semolini has been to see us once, but he really isn't very interesting."

"Ah, but still you're able to say that. I sha'n't be able to say, 'I met Semolini the other day, and, do you know, he's such a disappointment.'"

"Well, I couldn't help it, Bevan," murmured Miss Belvoir, smiling.

"No, I know you couldn't help it. Of course you couldn't help it. That's just it—you never expected the man. I went to lunch with another liar last week—I beg your pardon, Miss Belvoir—who asked me to meet Dusé. She was so sorry she couldn't come at the last minute. She sent a telegram. Well, all I ask is, let me see the telegram."

"But you couldn't; he 'phoned," objected Miss Belvoir.

"So you *say*," returned the young man, as he passed a cup of tea to Bertha.

"Will you have China tea and lemon and be smart, or India tea and milk and sugar and enjoy it? I don't mind owning that I like stewed tea—I like a nice comfortable washer-woman's cup of tea myself. Well, I suppose we're all going to the Indian ball at the Albert Hall. What are you all going as? I suppose Miss Belvoir's going as a nautch-girl, or a naughty girl or something."

"I'm going as a Persian dancer," said Miss Belvoir.

"I'm not going as anything," said Bertha. "I hate fancy balls. One takes such a lot of trouble and then people look only at their own dresses. If you want to dress up for yourself, you'd enjoy it just as much if you dressed up alone, I think."

"Well, of course it's not so much fun for women," said Mr. Fairfield. "You are always more or less in fancy dress; it's no change for you. But for us it is fun. The last one I went to I had a great success as a forget-me-not. Miss Belvoir and I met an elephant, an enormous creature, galumphing along, knocking every-body down, and wasn't it clever of me? I recognised it! 'Good heavens!' I exclaimed, 'this must be the Mitchells!' And so it turned out to be. Mr. Mitchell was one leg, Mrs. Mitchell the other, two others were their great friends and their little nephew was the trunk. Frightfully uncomfortable, but they did attract a great deal of attention. They nearly died of the stuffiness, but they took a prize. My friend Linsey usually takes a prize, though he always contrives some agonising torture for himself. The last time he was a letter-box, and he was simply dying of thirst and unable to move. I saved his life by pouring some champagne down the slit for the letters, on the chance. Another friend of mine who was dressed in a real suit of armour had to be lifted into the taxi, and when he arrived home he couldn't get out. When he at last persuaded the cabman to carry him to his door—it was six o'clock in the morning—the man said, 'Oh, never mind, sir, we've had gentlemen worse than this!' And the poor fellow hadn't had a single drop or crumb the whole evening, because his visor was down and he couldn't move his arm to lift it up. If you went as anything, Mrs. Kellynch, you ought to be a China Shepherdess. I never saw anyone so exactly like one."

"And what ought I to go as?" asked Madeline.

"You would look your best as a Florentine page," replied Mr. Fairfield. "Or both of you would look very nice as late Italians."

"I'm afraid we shall be late Englishwomen unless we go now," said Bertha. "I can only stay a very few minutes to-day, Miss Belvoir."

They persuaded her to remain a little longer, and Mr. Fairfield continued to chatter on during the remainder of their visit. He did not succeed in persuading them to join in making up the party for the Indian ball.

CHAPTER XXXI

MARY'S PLAN

MARY was so terrified that Nigel might keep his threat altogether and really leave her permanently that she made less opposition than he expected. She felt instinctively that it was her only chance of getting him back. She could see when he really meant a thing, and this time it was evident he intended to follow out his scheme, and she could not help reflecting that it might have been very much worse. How much more angry many husbands might have been! On the whole she had been let off fairly lightly. There was this much of largeness in Nigel's nature that he could not labour a point, or nag, or scold, or bully. He was really shocked and disgusted, besides being very angry at what she had done, and he did not at all like to dwell on it. He was even grateful that she spared him discussions of the subject, and sincerely thankful that she had admitted it. All men with any generosity in their temperament are disarmed by frankness, and most irritated by untruth. He wondered at her daring, and when she humbly owned she saw how dreadful it was —that she saw it in the right light and would never be tempted to do anything of the sort again—he was glad to forgive her. But he wanted to go away and forget it, and he certainly made up his mind to make the whole affair an excuse for having more freedom. He had never been away without her for more than a day, and he looked forward to it with great pleasure. He determined to let his journey help to cure him of his passion for Bertha, though it seemed at present an almost impossible task.

He was resolved to strike when the iron was hot, and to get away while she was in this docile mood. She was gentle and quiet and seemed very unhappy, but made no objections to his plans; she would not, perhaps, have minded his leaving her for a day or two, since she felt uncomfortable and in the wrong, but she dreaded his being away for weeks. He said he would join Rupert at Venice; and this she rather preferred, as Rupert was known to be a quiet, steady, studious young man.

But when the last moment came and the packed trunks were put on the cab, he had said good-bye to her and the children and that last terrible bang of the hall door resounded in her heart, she could not look out of the window in her usual place. She had felt the agony known to all loving hearts, the conviction that a traveller is already at a distance before he goes. He is no longer with her when his thoughts are with stations and tickets—indeed the real parting is long before he starts. Then the unconscious sparkle of pleasure in his eyes as he imagines himself away! He had gone already before he went; she did not want to see the last of him. She went up to her room and locked the door, and threw herself on the sofa in a terrible fit of despair and jealousy. Jealousy still, that was her great fear of his going away. He would forget her and be unfaithful, she thought. . . .

She suffered terribly that evening, and the next day resolved to take a somewhat singular step. If she had been doing Bertha an injustice, as it seemed, if Bertha was not seeing him at all, why should she not go and see her? She felt instinctively that besides getting the truth out of her, and perhaps apologising for what had happened at the party, Bertha might give her some advice. Everyone said she was so kind and clever. She decided not to write, but she rang up on the telephone and asked if Bertha would receive her at three o'clock. She felt a strange curiosity, a longing to see her. She received the answer, Mrs. Kellynch would be delighted to see her at any time in the afternoon.

CHAPTER XXXII

PRIVATE FIREWORKS AT THE PICKERINGS'

"I SAY, Clifford, when is your birthday?"

This momentous question was asked of Clifford with the liveliest interest by Cissy Pickering, a remarkably pretty little girl of about his own age.

They were in the gigantic and gorgeous apartment set apart as a playroom for the young Pickerings in Hamilton Place, Park Lane, and arranged partly as a gymnasium—it had all the necessities—partly as a schoolroom. It contained a magnificent dolls' house fitted up with Louis Quinze furniture and illuminated with real electric light; a miniature motor car in which two small people could drive themselves with authentic petrol round and round the polished floor; a mechanical rocking-horse; a miniature billiard-table and croquet set; a gramophone; cricket on the hearth, roller-skates; a pianola, and countless other luxuries.

Decorated by illustrations of fairy tales on the walls, it was altogether a delightful room; made for all a child could want.

It is all very well to say that children are happier with mud pies and rag dolls than with these elaborate delights. There may be something in this theory, but when their amusements are carried to such a point of luxurious and imaginative perfection it certainly gives them great and even unlimited enjoyment at the time. Whether such indulgence and realisation of youthful dreams have a good effect on the character in later life is a different question. At any rate, to go to tea with the Pickerings was the dream of all their young friends and gave them much to think of and long for, while it gave to the young host and hostess immense gratification and material pride.

"My birthday? Oh, I don't know—oh, it's on the twenty-seventh May," said Clifford, who was far more shy of the young lady than of her mother.

"Fancy! Just fancy! and mine's on the twenty-eighth June! *Isn't* it funny!"

Cissy was surprised at almost everything. It added to her popularity.

"Not particularly."

"Oh, Clifford!"

"You must be born some time or other, I mean," he said, wriggling his head and twisting his feet, as he did when he felt embarrassed. Miss Pickering made him feel embarrassed because she asked so many direct personal questions, seemed so interested and surprised at everything, and volunteered so much private —but, it seemed to him, unimportant—information.

"My name is Cecilia Muriel Margaret Pickering. My birthday's on the twenty-eighth June, and Eustace's birthday is on the fifteenth February. Isn't it funny?"

"No, not at all," said Clifford.

"His name is Eustace Henry John Pickering, after father. At least John's after father and Henry's after grandpapa—I mean, mummy's father, you know. Eustace is just a fancy name—a name mummy thought of. Do you like it?"

"Not much."

"Oh, Clifford! Why not?"

"Well, it's rather a queer name."

"Do you call him Eustace?"

"I call him Pickering, of course," said Clifford. "At school we don't know each other's Christian names."

"Oh! . . . Did you know mine before you came here, Clifford?"

"No. I only knew he had a kiddy sister, but he didn't tell me your name."

She looked rather crushed. Cissy was a lovely child with golden hair, parted on one side, and a dainty white and pink dress like a doll. Cissy was in love with Clifford, but Clifford was in love with her mother. This simple nursery tragedy may sound strange, but as a matter of fact it is a kind of thing that happens every day. Similar complications are to be found in almost every schoolroom.

"I hope you don't mind my saying that," said Clifford, who began to be sorry for her. "About your being a kid. It doesn't matter a bit—for a girl."

"Oh, Clifford! No, I don't mind." She smiled at him, consoled. "Eustace will soon be home. He's gone to get something."

"Oh, good."

"Do you mind his not being here yet?"

"No, not a bit."

"You told me you had something to show me," said the little girl. "You've been writing poetry. I *should* so like to see it."

He blushed and said: "I've brought it. But I don't think it's any good. I don't think I'll show it to you."

"Oh, please, please, *please*, do!"

"You'll go telling everyone. Girls always do."

"I promise, I *swear* I won't! Not a soul. Not even mummy. I never tell Eustace's secrets."

"I should think not! Now mind you don't, then. Will you, Cissy?"

"Oh, do go on, dear Clifford; because when Eustace is here we shall have to play games—'Happy Families' or something—and I sha'n't have another chance. I believe he's got some joke on. I hear you've written a play. Have you?"

"Well, I began an historical play," said Clifford, who was beginning to think a little sister with proper respect for one might be rather a luxury, "but I chucked it. I found it was rather slow. So then I tried to write a poem. But I'm not going to grow up and be one of those rotten poets with long hair, that you read of. Don't think that."

"Aren't you? Oh, that's right. What are you going to be, Clifford?"

"Oh! I think I shall be an inventor or an explorer, and go out after the North or South Pole, or shoot lions."

"Oh! How splendid! Won't you take me? I'd *love* to come!"

He smiled. "It wouldn't do for girls."

"But I sha'n't be a girl then. I'll be grown-up. *Do* let me come!"

"We'll see. Don't bother."

"Well! Show me the poem," she said, for she already had the instinct to see that it pleased him and interested him much more to show her what he was doing at present than to make promises and plans about her future.

They went and sat on the delightful wide-cushioned window-seat. Clifford pulled out of his pocket a crumpled paper, covered with pencil marks. He curled himself up, and Cissy curled herself up beside him and looked over his shoulder.

He began: "I'm afraid this one's no use—no earthly—— I say, Cissy, take your hair out of my eyes."

She shook it back and sat a little farther off, with her eyes and mouth open as he read in a rather gruff voice:

"Sonnet."

"What's a sonnet, Clifford?"

He was rather baffled. "This is."

He went on:

"'*The day when first I saw*
Her standing by the door,
I was taken by surprise
By her pretty blue eyes,
And then I thought her hair
So very fair
That I felt inclined to sing
About Mrs. Pickering.'"

"Lovely! How beautiful!" exclaimed Cissy, like a true woman. "But Mrs. Pickering! Fancy! Does it mean mummy?"

"Why, yes. As a matter of fact it certainly *does.*"

"Oh, Clifford! *How* clever! How splendid! But mustn't she know it?"

"Oh no. I'd rather not. At any rate, not now."

"I wish it was to me!" exclaimed the child. "Then you needn't be so shy about it. Why don't you change it to me? Look here—like this. Say:

"'I felt inclined to sing
About Cissy Pickering.'

Cissy instead of *Mrs.!*"

"Oh no, my dear. That wouldn't do at all. It isn't done. You can't alter a sonnet to another person. If it came to that I'd sooner write one to you as well, some time or another, when you're older."

"Oh, *do*, *dear* Cliff! I *should* love it."

"All right. Perhaps I will some day. But, you see, just now I want to do the one about *her.*"

"It's very nice and polite of you," she said in a doubting voice. "But you said you'd done some more."

"Rather. So I have. You mustn't think it's cheek, you know, if I call your mother by her

Christian name in the poetry. It's only for the rhyme."

Blushing and apologetically he read aloud in his gruff, shy voice:

"'*Geraldine, Geraldline,*
She has the nicest face I have ever seen,
She did not say
Until the other day
That I might call her Geraldine,
And I think she is like a Queen.'

"As a matter of fact she never said it at all," said the boy, folding it up. "That's only because it's poetry. And I only used her name for the rhyme."

"Yes, I see. You're very clever!"

"Don't you see any faults in it? I wish you'd tell me straight out exactly what you think, if you see anything wrong," said Clifford, like all young writers who think they are pining for criticism but are really yearning for praise. "I would like," he said, "for you to find any fault you possibly could! Say exactly what you really mean."

He really thought he meant it.

"Well, I don't see *one* fault! I think it's perfect," replied Cissy, like all intelligent women in love with the writer. Her instinct warned her against finding any fault. Had she found any it would have been the only thing Clifford would have thought she happened to be wrong about. As it was, his opinion of her judgment and general mental capacity went up enormously, and he decided that she was a very clever kid. A decent little girl too, and not at all bad looking.

"But aren't they a little short, Cissy?" he asked.

"Perhaps they are. But you can easily make them longer, can't you?"

"Oh yes, rather, of course I can."

"Don't you want mummy to see them?"

"Oh no, I don't think I do; wouldn't she laugh at me?"

"Oh no, I'm sure she wouldn't, Clifford. She's coming to have tea with us to-night."

"Well, mind you don't tell," he said threateningly.

"Of course, I won't. You can trust me. I say, Clifford."

"Well?"

"What do you think I used to want to do?"

"Haven't the slightest idea."

She hesitated a moment. "Shall I tell you?"

"If you like."

"Well, I used to want to marry Henry Ainley!"

"Did you, though," said Clifford, not very interested.

"Yes. But I don't now."

"Don't you, though?"

"No, not the least bit."

"Did he want to marry you?" asked Clifford. This idea occured to him as being conversational, but he was still not interested.

"Oh, good gracious, no!" she exclaimed. "Of course not! rather not! Why, he doesn't know me. And if he did he would think I was a little girl."

"Well, so you are," said Clifford.

"I know. Shall I tell you why I don't want to marry Henry Ainley any more?"

"You can if you want to." These matrimonial schemes seemed to bore him, but he thought he ought to endure them as a matter of fair play, as she had listened to his poetry.

"Well, I don't care so much about marrying him now, because I should like to marry you!"

"Me! Oh, good Lord, I don't want to be engaged, thanks."

"Oh, Clifford, do!"

"None of the chaps at school are engaged. It isn't done. Being engaged is rot. Pickering isn't engaged."

"Yes; but I don't see why we shouldn't," she said, pouting.

"Well, I do, and I sha'n't be."

"But mightn't you later on, when we're older?" she implored.

"Why, no, I shouldn't think so. Why, your mother would be very angry. You're only twelve. You're not out. You can't be engaged before you're out. Your mother would think it awful cheek of me."

"Well, I won't say anything more about it now," she said. "But, Clifford, will you, *perhaps*, *when* I am out?"

"Oh, good Lord! What utter bosh. How do I know what I'll do when you're out?"

She began to look tearful.

"Oh, well, all right. I'll see. Perhaps I may. Mind, I don't promise."

He was thinking that if he refused her irrevocably and unconditionally he might not be asked to the house again. And he liked going on account of Pickering, Mrs. Pickering, and the house.

"Look here," he said after a moment's pause. "Let's forget all about this. I don't think your mother would like it."

"You think so much of my mother," she answered.

"Well, I should think so, don't you?"

"Oh yes, Clifford, I love her, of course."

"Well, then, don't you want me to like her?"

"Oh yes; but not much more than me."

"Oh, well, I can't help that," he said very decidedly.

She looked subdued.

"Then you do like me a little bit too, Clifford?"

"Yes, of course. I say, don't worry."

"All right, I beg your pardon, Clifford. . . . Oh, there's Eustace!"

His step was heard. When his friends were there his sister called him Pickering, not to be out of it.

"Won't you kiss me to show you're not cross with me, Clifford?"

"Yes, if you like, my dear. But we're not engaged, you know."

"Right-o," she answered.

He kissed her hurriedly and Eustace came in. Eustace was a big dark thin boy of fourteen, not good-looking or like his sister in any way, but with a very pleasant humorous expression. He was remarkably clever at school, and his reports were, with regard to work, quite unusually high. Conduct was not so satisfactory, though he was popular both with boys and masters. His two hobbies were chemistry and practical jokes. Unfortunately the clear distinction between the two was not always sufficiently marked; the one merged too frequently into the other. Hence occasional trouble.

Eustace had his arms full of parcels, which looked rather exciting. He informed his delighted sister and friend that they were going to have private fireworks on the balcony.

"Gracious, how ripping!" cried Clifford. "But it isn't the fifth of November."

"Who on earth ever said it was?"

"Is it anybody's birthday?" asked Cissy.

"I daresay," said Pickering. "Sure to be."

"But you don't know that it's anybody's birthday for a fact, do you?"

"Yes, I do. It's a dead cert that it's somebody's. Somebody's born every day. It's probably several people's birthday."

"But you don't know whose?"

"No. I don't know whose and I don't want to; what does it matter? Who cares?"

They both laughed heartily. It was so like Pickering! That was Pickering all over to give an exhibition of fireworks in honour of the birthday of somebody he didn't know anything about, or in honour of its not being the fifth November.

"But will mummy mind? Won't she be afraid?"

"She won't mind, because she won't know. And she won't be afraid because she and father are going out to dinner and they won't hear anything about it until all the danger's over.

I've got rockets and Bengal lights and all sorts of things here."

"But suppose they catch fire to the curtains on the balcony and we have a fire-escape here," suggested Cissy.

"Well, and wouldn't that be ripping?"

They admitted that it would.

"Have you ever been down a fire-escape, Clifford?" asked Pickering.

"Me? Down a fire-escape? Wait a minute, let me think. No, no. Now I come to think of it, upon my word, I don't think I ever have. Not down a *fire-escape*."

"Ah, I thought not," said Pickering knowingly, as if he had spent his life doing nothing else. "No, you wouldn't have."

"Well, have you?"

"Me?" said Pickering. "Well, I don't know that I have, *exactly*. But I know all about it. Besides I once drove to a fire with one of the firemen. It was jolly."

"But you're not going to give a fire-escape performance to-night, are you? I thought you were only going to have fireworks."

"Yes, of course, that's all, and there's no danger really. How surprised the people in the street will be when they see those ripping rockets go whizzing up! I daresay we shall have a crowd round us."

"But I say, Eustace. Won't mummy say it's *vulgar*?"

"What's vulgar?"

"Why, to have fireworks. She says we oughtn't to attract too much attention and do anything ostentatious. She often says so."

"Oh, my dear, that's all right. These are *private* fireworks! No one will know about it."

"But you'll have to tell Wenham," said Cissy.

Wenham was a confidential butler who helped Pickering out of many scrapes.

"Of course I shall tell Wenham; at least, I shall as soon as they have started. Now shut up about it. Here's mummy."

Pretty Mrs. Pickering joined them at tea, played games with them—they did some delightful charades—and amused them and herself until it was time for her to go and dress for dinner, leaving Clifford more enchanted with her than ever.

About a quarter to eight the children had the house more or less to themselves. Cissy's governess had a holiday and the aged nurse (who had no sort of control over Pickering) was the only person there who had even a shadow of authority. She was to see that Cissy didn't play wild games, and went to bed at half-past eight, but as a matter of fact the aged nurse did neither. Cissy stayed with the boys as long as they would allow her. At last the joyous moment arrived, they went on the balcony and Pickering started his first rocket. Cissy, a little frightened, clung to Clifford.

"Suppose we have a crowd round the house," she murmured.

"You see how easy it is," Pickering said. "Anyone with a little sense can do it. Now! Now, Cissy! get out of the way!"

They waited and waited. But, alas! nothing happened. He tried again and yet again, but it turned out a failure, the sort of tragedy that is more disappointing than any danger or even any accident. . . . It fell completely flat.

*

There must have been something the matter with the infernal fireworks. It couldn't have been Pickering not knowing how to do them.

That was impossible, simply because Pickering always knew how to do everything.

The wretched man who sold them to him must have cheated.

It was a terrible *fiasco.* Not a single one of the rotten things went off. The most awful thing happened that could happen in life. After great fear, hope, suspense, excitement and joy, *the squibs were damp!*

Nothing went off. Nothing happened. As to the Bengal fire, nothing was ever seen of it but some damp paper and a very horrible scent. Certainly there was no vulgarity about it, no ostentation, except the perfume. The fireworks were as private as they could possibly be!

"At any rate," said Cissy, trying to console her guest, "perhaps it's better than if the house had caught fire and we had all been burnt up!"

They weren't so very sure. It wouldn't have been so flat.

Then Pickering made an attempt to imply that the whole thing was simply a practical joke of his.

"Well, if it is," said Clifford to himself, "by Jove, if it is—it's the greatest success I've ever seen in my life!"

CHAPTER XXXIII

NIGEL ABROAD

NIGEL "ran across" Rupert in Paris—Englishmen who are acquainted with each other always do meet in Paris—and they agreed to dine together. Each was pleased to see the other, not so much for each other's own sake, but for the pleasure of associations. The sight of Rupert reminded Nigel of one of the pleasantest evenings in his life—that evening they had spent at the Russian Ballet. Bertha had sat next to him. Bertha had been delightful. She had looked lovely and laughed at his jokes, and had been all brightness and amiability—it had been before the first shadow, the first thought of *arrière pensée* had risen in her mind to cloud her light heart. And he at that time, with what he saw now to be his dense stupidity, had believed that she was beginning to like him, that she was even on the way to get to care for him in time if he managed with great tact and did not annoy Percy nor seem wanting in deference for him, and above all if he did not give it away about Mary's jealousy. He always knew that if Bertha once learnt that, it would be fatal to his hopes. She was never to know it.

And now everything had come out, everything had gone wrong in the most horrible, hideous way. It had all gone off like young Pickering's fireworks. When he remembered that dreadful scene at the party it made him shudder. How hopelessly stupid he had been to persuade her to come! How could he have been so idiotic? Looking at Rupert reminded him of the delightful little meetings and talks he had had with Bertha about him and Madeline. How charmingly grateful and delighted she had been at his offering to help her and smooth away the difficulties by diplomacy. And this was how he had done it! Madeline was now engaged to nobody.

Bertha knew all about the jealousy and had been exposed to insults. And Percy knew even more about it than she did. Talk of diplomacy! Nigel must have been indeed a poor diplomatist, since, without having ever done the slightest harm or indeed really said a word of love to Bertha, he had yet brought her husband down upon him, forbidding him the house and sending him to the devil. That was diplomacy, wasn't it? and as to success, she regarded him with indifference bordering on aversion and was clearly madly in love with that dull uninteresting Percy. All (Nigel admitted), all his own stupidity. Whether or not wickedness is punished in another world, there can be no doubt that stupidity and folly is most decidedly punished in this.

But then, could he help it that Mary went behind his back and wrote the most dreadful letters, that she had this terrible mania for writing letters? But if he had been so very clever and diplomatic he would somehow or another have prevented it. Oh yes, there was no doubt he was a fool, and he had without doubt been made supremely ridiculous. He was well aware that he was ridiculous.

Rupert Denison liked Nigel, but he had no idea how intimate he was with Nigel. In other words he hadn't the faintest idea how well Nigel knew him. And this is a case which happens every day owing to the present custom of confidential gossip; and is too frequently rather unfairly arranged through the intimate friendship of women. For example, Madeline, regarding Bertha as the most confidential of sisters, told her every little thing, showed her every letter, and had no shadow of a secret from her in word or thought. Bertha was almost equally confiding, except than an older married woman is never quite so frank with a girl friend—there must always be certain reservations. Bertha was an intimate friend of Nigel and practically told *him* every little thing—he was "the sort of man you could tell everything to," he was interested, amused, and gave excellent advice. The result was obvious; very little about Rupert and his private romance with Madeline was unrevealed to Nigel.

Nigel felt inclined to smile when he remembered all he had heard. Rupert, on the other hand, was not "the sort of man you could tell everything to"; he therefore had no confidential women friends and knew nothing at all about Nigel. For all he knew, he was just as much as ever *l'ami de la maison* at Percy's house.

At the very end of the dinner, which was a very pleasant one, during which Nigel had been sparkling and Rupert a little quiet, Nigel suddenly "felt it in his bones," as Bertha used to say—dear Bertha, she used to declare that her bones were so peculiarly and remarkably sensitive to anything of interest—Nigel felt, as I say, Rupert was longing to talk about Madeline.

He therefore led the conversation to her, remarked how quiet she had been of late, and told him various things about her.

"Did she ever mention me?" asked Rupert, as he looked down at his wineglass.

"Oh yes, rather."

"What did she say?"

"She said," replied Nigel, "that she was jolly glad she never saw you now and that you were a silly rotter!"

"I recognise Miss Madeline's style," replied Rupert with a smile, as he rose from the table.

CHAPTER XXXIV

MOONA

LIKE all cultivated people, particularly those who attach much importance to pleasure and amusement, variety, art, and the play, Nigel was very fond of Paris; it always pleased him to go there; and yet he doubted if he were quite as fond of it in reality as he was in theory. The best acting, the best cooking, the best millinery in the world was to be found in Paris; and yet Nigel wasn't sure that he didn't enjoy those things more when he got them in London—that he enjoyed French cooking best in an English restaurant, and even a French play at an English theàtre. Certainly Paris was the centre of art. Nigel was fond of pictures, and he amused himself more with a few young French artists whom he happened to know living here than with anybody else in the city; and yet when he went back to London he sometimes felt that the recollection of it, the chatter of studios, the slang of the critics, even the whole sense and sound of Paris gave him a little the recollection as of a huge cage of monkeys. Like most modern Englishmen, he talked disparagingly about British hypocrisy, Anglo-Saxon humbug, English stiffness and London fog; and yet, after all, he missed and valued these very things. Wasn't the fog and the hypocrisy—one was the symbol of the other—weren't all these things the very charm of London? Fog and hypocrisy—that is to say, shadow, convention, decency—these were the very things that lent to London its poetry and romance.

Everything in Paris, it was true, was picturesque, everything had colour and form, everything made a picture. But it was all too obvious; everything was all there ready for one's amusement, ready for one's pleasure. People were too obliging, too willing. And the men! Well, Nigel was far more of a *viveur*, of a lover of pleasure than ninety-nine Englishmen out of a hundred, yet he found too much of that point of view among the men he came across in Paris. From boys to old gentlemen, from the artists to a certain set among the *haute finance*—of whom he had some acquaintances—from the sporting young sprig of the Faubourg to the son of the sham jeweller in the Rue de Rivoli—all, without a single exception, seemed to think of nothing else but pleasure, in other words, of *les petites femmes*. For that—paying attention more or less serious to *les petites femmes*—seemed the one real idea of pleasure. Of this point of view Nigel certainly grew very tired, and he marvelled at the wonderful energy, the unflagging interest in the same eternal subject.

They said, and of course thought, that there was nothing so charming as a French woman, particularly the Parisienne; but, except on one point, he was not entirely inclined to agree. This point was their dress. Their dress was delightful, their fashion was an art, and it had great, real charm. In whatever walk of life they were placed they were always exquisitely dressed. Nigel appreciated this sartorial gift, it was an art he understood and that amused, but weren't they on the whole—also in every walk of life—a little too much arranged, overdone, too much *maquillées*; weren't their faces too white, their lips too red, their hats too new? They knew how to put on their clothes to perfection, but he was not sure that he didn't prefer these beautiful clothes not quite so well put on; he thought he liked to see the pretty French dress put on a little wrong on a pretty Englishwoman; and then he thought of Bertha, of course. Nowhere in Paris was there anything quite like Bertha, that pink and white English complexion, that abundant fair hair, the natural flower-like look.

Of course Bertha was unusually clever, lively and charming; she was not stiff or prim, she was very exceptional, but distinctly English, and he admired her more than all the Parisiennes in the world. Besides, he thought, one got very tired of them. When they *were bourgeoises* they were so extremely *bourgeoises*; when they were smart they were so excessively *snob*. Perhaps it was through having seen a good deal of them for a little while that he met a compatriot of his with unexpected gratification.

He was walking with one of his artist friends on the boulevard when, to his great surprise, the artist was stopped by a young lady walking alone who evidently knew him. She was dressed in a very tight blue serge coat and skirt, she had black bandeaux of hair over her ears, from which depended imitation coral earrings. She had shoes with white spats, and a very small hat squashed over her eyes. She did not look in the least French. He knew her at once. It was the girl whose artistic education Rupert had at one time undertaken. It was Moona Chivvey.

"Ah! Miss Chivvey! What a pleasure! And what are you doing here?"

She replied that she and her friend, Mimsie Sutton, had taken a little studio and were studying art together with a number of other

English and American girls with a great artist.

Nigel's friend left his arm and went away. Nigel strolled on with Miss Chivvey.

"And are you here quite alone with no chaperon," asked Nigel, with that momentary sort of brotherly feeling of being shocked that an Englishman nearly always feels when he sees a compatriot behaving unconventionally in a foreign land.

"Chaperon! Oh! come off the roof," replied the young lady in her boisterous manner, which he saw had not at all toned down. "Of course I'm being chaperoned by Miss Sutton. I'm staying with Mimsie. Mother couldn't come, and didn't want me to come, but there's no hope of learning art in London; it's simply *hopeless*. You see we're serious, Mr. Hillier, we're studying really hard. We're going to do big things. Mimsie's a genius. I'm not; but I'm industrious. I'm a tremendous worker. Oh, I shall do something yet!"

She was full of fire and enthusiasm, and continued to give him an immense quantity of information. He listened with interest and thought it rather touching. Of course she was genuine and believed in herself; equally, of course, she had no sort of talent. She was in a position in which no girl in her own class could be placed who was not English, except an American, and then it wouldn't be the same thing. No doubt she knew thoroughly well how to take care of herself, and most likely there was no need, even, that she should. Still, he thought it was rather pathetic that she should leave her parents and a thoroughly comfortable home in Camden Hill, in order to live in a wretchedly uncomfortable studio—he was sure it was wretchedly uncomfortable—and have a dull life with other depressing girls —all for the cultivation of a gift that was purely imaginary.

"You must come and dine with me to-night, won't you, Miss Chivvey?"

She was rather pretty, rather amusing, and she was English. He liked talking English again.

"Well, I should like to very much, Mr. Hillier. Is your wife here?"

"No; she's going to Felixtowe in a week or two with the children, and I'm going to join her there. I'm quite alone, so you must take pity on me. Must we have your friend Miss Sutton too?" he asked.

"Oh no—I don't think it's necessary; it will be a change to go out without her. You see, here I am a worker and a Bohemian," she explained. "I don't go in for chaperons. I'm not social here!"

"Besides, I'm English. You're all right with me," he returned in his most charming way. "Have you many English friends here?"

He wanted to find out whether she was seeing Rupert; he soon discovered she was not, and he determined not to tell her of the presence of that young man. They might make it up, and Nigel thought it would be far better for Rupert to come back to Madeline. He was sure she was his real taste. And he still wanted to please Bertha.

They dined in a small but particularly excellent restaurant. She seemed to enjoy herself immensely, and grew every moment more confidential. Nigel tried not to flirt. He had no intention of doing so, and, had they met in London, would not have dreamt of such a thing; but meeting an English girl placed as she was gave a tinge of adventure and romance to his taking her out.

She told him she had no flirtations and cared for no man in the world. He then led the conversation gradually to Rupert Denison. It did not take long for her to work herself up to give him a somewhat highly coloured version of their quarrel, which amused him. It ended with "and so I never saw him again."

"I can't see that you have any real grievance, I must say. He seems to have been very nice to you, taken you out a great deal, and gone to see you pretty often. Did he not make love to you?"

"Never, never, never," she replied. "He was just like a brother, or, rather, a sort of schoolmaster."

"Then I believe that's what made you angry," he replied.

"Indeed it isn't. At any rate, if it was a little, I assure you I'm not in love with him."

He laughed, teased her about it, and now he found that she wished to go home. Feeling he ought not to take advantage of her position here, he was exceedingly respectful, and drove her to her flat, not before she had consented to dine and go to the theatre with him the next day.

"That sort of girl is rather difficult to understand," he thought, as he drove away from the studio. "Perhaps now she's thinking me a fool as she thought Rupert."

However, he remembered *he* was married. He looked forward to the next evening with interest. At least Miss Chivvey was different from other people. One wasn't quite sure of her, and that fact had its attraction. She was really very good-looking too, very young, had beautiful eyes and teeth, and the high spirits of youth and health and enthusiasm. Pity she thought she could draw. How much better if she had gone in for first-rate plain cooking! He was sure she could learn that—if it was really plain.

Next day he sent her a few flowers. After all, an Englishman must be gallant to his countrywoman; but the next evening he thought she met him with a slightly cooler air and even with a little embarrassment. This melted away before the end of the evening.

He then took her to the theatre in a little box. He was careful to choose a piece that he would have taken his own sister to see, but he forgot that he would not have let his own sister go to see it with a married man and no chaperon.

His manner was becoming a shade more tender than was necessary, and he was sitting perhaps a shade nearer to her than was absolutely required, when, looking up, he saw two young men in the stalls, one of whom was looking at him and his companion with very great interest through an opera-glass. It was Rupert.

Moona had not seen him, and Nigel now became aware of a distinct anxiety that she should not. He was rather sorry he had come: it might give Rupert a mistaken impression. It was not right to compromise her. He would explain, of course, the next day. But it was annoying to have to explain, and he would have explained anyhow. Nigel greatly disliked getting the credit, or, rather, the discredit, of something he did not deserve.

He pretended to be bored with the play, and persuaded her to come and have an ice at a quiet and respectable place before she saw Rupert. She went in high spirits and great innocence.

When they left Nigel said: "Do you know that I oughtn't to have taken you there to-night? It was wrong of me. If anyone had seen us there they would probably have mistaken our relations."

She gave her boisterous laugh and said: "I see. Well, you would have had all the credit and none of the trouble."

"You mean," he replied, "that I should have had all the infamy and none of the satisfaction."

As they drove to the studio he took her hand and said: "One kiss."

"Certainly not," she replied, taking it away. "Certainly not. Do you want me to be sorry I came out with you?"

"I should like you to be glad," he replied. "Never mind, Miss Chivvey, forgive me. I won't ask you out again."

"Why not? Haven't I been nice?"

"Very nice. Too nice, too charming, too dangerous." He kissed her hand respectfully. "Good-bye. I'm angry with myself."

"Never mind, I'll forgive you," she laughed flippantly.

He drove away. Yes, one loses one's bearings travelling about alone, taking *jeunes filles* to the theatre who live alone in Paris, say anything, have no chaperons, and are prudes all the time.

"Confound it. I've made a fool of myself. But I must go and see Rupert."

He lunched with that young man that day and told him word for word what had passed, even to the incident in the cab.

He need not have been so expansive nor have humbled himself so much.

Rupert had not for a moment misconstrued their presence at the theatre.

Also he was not in the least surprised about the incident in the cab.

Rupert was on the whole irritating. Nigel was glad to leave him.

CHAPTER XXXV

TWO WOMEN

BERTHA was very much surprised at Mary's wishing to see her. She thought it most extraordinary and was much inclined to refuse, remembering the strangely insulting way Mary had behaved at her party. Nigel had apologised indeed; had implored for forgiveness; and she had written to say it was forgotten. But it is not an easy thing to forget.

Percy had given a mild version of his interview with Nigel. He had also told her now about the destroyed letters. Bertha was certainly vexed that she had not been told before. It would have, at least, prevented her going to the party. However, she was soon tired of the subject and agreed with Percy not to mention it again. Bertha was, as she said herself, nothing of a harpist. She could not go on playing on one string. She made up her mind to forget it. She had begun to do so when Mary's telephone message reached her.

Bertha was sitting by the fire when Mary was shown in. She looked at her most serene, her calmest and prettiest. It was not in her nature to bear malice nor even to be angry for more than a few hours about anything. By the end of that time she was always inclined to see the humorous side of anything, and to see that it was of less importance than appeared. She had already laughed several times to herself at the mere thought of the absurdity of a hostess asking one to her house and then behaving as Mary had done. Also she saw a comic—though pathetic—side to the typewritten letters. But it was painful, too, and she would very much rather have avoided this visit from Mrs. Hillier. It must be embarrassing for her, at least, and could hardly be other than disagreeable.

Mary came in looking very pale and rather untidy. In the excitement of her mind and her general perturbation she had come out with two left-handed gloves, and during the whole of her visit endeavoured to force a left hand into a right-hand glove. It was maddening to watch her.

Just as she started to go to see Bertha, poor Mary had gone to her toilet-table and put what she supposed to be powder lavishly on her nose without again looking in the glass. It was red rouge—the reddest and brightest. Although she afterwards rubbed a little of it off, she never saw herself in the glass again before starting. The result of this was to give her that touch of the grotesque that is so fatal to any scene of a serious nature but that in this case appealed to Bertha's kindness and sympathy rather than her sense of humour.

"How are you, Mrs. Hillier? I have really hardly met you to speak to until to-day."

"Good-morning, Mrs. Kellynch. . . . It was kind of you to let me come."

Mary sat down awkwardly and began to put her left hand into the right-hand glove. She sat near the light, and Bertha saw that she had been covering her face with what she supposed to be powder, but what was nothing else than carmine.

Should she tell her?

Could she let her remain in ignorance of this until afterwards? She would find it out when she went home.

"I want to speak to you very much, Mrs. Kellynch. . . . It is very awkward, but I feel I must."

"Have some tea first," said Bertha, and while she poured it out and passed it to Mrs. Hillier she felt she could no longer leave her in ignorance of her appearance.

She pointed to the silver looking-glass that stood on a small table, and said: "Mrs. Hillier, just look at that. I fancy you've put something on your face by mistake. Do forgive me!"

Mary gave a shriek.

"Good heavens, how horrible! I must have put rouge on instead of powder! I look like a comic actor!"

Both of them laughed, and this rather cleared the air.

"It was very good of you to tell me," said Mary. "Thank you. It's so like me! When I'm agitated I become too appallingly absent-minded for words. That's the sort of thing I do. How you must sneer—I mean, laugh at me, Mrs. Kellynch!"

"Indeed not! What an idea. It could happen to anyone."

"Well, I came to see you for two reasons. One is this: Mrs. Kellynch, I want to beg your pardon. I'm very, very sorry."

"For what, Mrs. Hillier?"

"For many things. I was horribly rude—I behaved shamefully at my party the other day. I must have been mad. I was so miserable." She said this in a low voice.

Bertha held out her hand. The poor girl—she was not much more—looked so miserable, and had just looked so absurd! It must have been such a humiliation to know that one had called on one's rival got up like a comedian—a singer of comic songs at the Pavilion.

"Mrs. Hillier, don't say any more. I quite forgive you, and will not think of it again. Don't let us talk of it any more. Have some more tea?"

"No, thank you, Mrs. Kellynch. This isn't all. I have something else to tell you, and then I want, if I may, to consult you. I did a dreadful, dreadful thing! I don't know how I could! Oh, when I see you—when I look at you and see how sweet and kind you are——"

Bertha, terrified that Mary would begin to cry and get hysterical, tried to stop her.

"Don't, Mrs. Hillier. Don't tell me any more. It might—I guess what you are going to say—I know it might have caused great trouble. But it didn't. So never mind. You were upset—didn't think."

"Oh no, Mrs. Kellynch; you must let me confess it. I sha'n't be at peace till I do. I want to tell—my husband—that I confessed and apologised. I actually wrote——"

"Really, all this is unnecessary. You are giving us both unnecessary pain," said Bertha. "I know it—I guess it. Won't you leave it at that? All traces of—the trouble were destroyed, and, if you want to be kind to me now, you'll not speak of it any more."

Mary had begun to cry, but she controlled herself, seeing it would please Bertha best.

"Very well, I'll say no more. Only do, *do* try to forgive me."

"I do with all my heart."

"Then you're angelic. Thank you." After a moment's pause, Mary put away her handkerchief.

"Have a cigarette," suggested Bertha, who hardly knew what to do to compose her agitated visitor.

"No, no, thank you. Mrs. Kellynch, may I really ask you a great, *great* favour?"

"Please do."

"May I consult you? I'm *so* miserable—I'm wretched. Nigel has gone away and left me!"

"Gone away."

"Yes."

"But he'll come back? Surely, he means to come back?"

"I *hope* so. But he never left me before. Never since we have been married! And I am miserable. What shall I do—what can I do to make him fond of me?"

This pathetic question brought tears to Bertha's eyes. She was truly sorry for the poor little creature.

"Is he angry with you then?"

"He's not exactly angry, now. He has been very kind. He has behaved beautifully. But he said he must go away for a time, and when he came back he would not refer to—to the subject of our quarrel again."

"Well, that's all right then. There is no cause for being unhappy. It's nothing his going away for a week or two."

"He says *six* weeks. Six long, dreadful weeks!"

"Even six weeks —it's nothing. After, you'll both be much happier, I'm sure," said Bertha consolingly. "Sometimes there is a sort of strain and a change is needed. It will be all right."

"But, Mrs. Kellynch, you don't know—you don't understand. I have always been so terribly, madly jealous. I have worried him into it. You see—I can't help it, I love him *so* much! I do love him. You can't imagine what it is!"

"Indeed I can!" cried Bertha. "I care *quite* as much for Percy. You can't think how much."

"Really and truly? But that's so different, because *he* cares quite as much for you."

"Indeed, I hope so," said Bertha seriously.

"Yes. But Nigel doesn't—he's kind, but I don't think he cares much about me. What shall I do?"

Bertha paused, deeply sorry. Then she said:

"Nonsense! Of course he does, but you—if you'll excuse my saying so—you seem to worry him, to bother him with imaginary grievances, with unjust suspicious. What man will bear that?"

"Then will you tell me what to do?" she asked, like a child.

"First, don't beg him to come back. Write kindly, unselfishly, cheerfully."

"Cheerfully! Oh, I can't."

"Yes; you must if you want it to be all right. What man wants to be deluged with tears and complaints? Dear Mrs. Hillier, I'm speaking as a genuine friend. I'm speaking frankly. I'm advising you as I would my own sister. Write to him cheerily, and take an interest in his doings, but not *too* great. Show less curiosity. Above all, no jealousy, no suspicions. It's the worst thing in the world."

"Is it? Go on, dear Mrs. Kellynch. Tell me more."

"Talk of the children—show interest in them—make him proud of them. There you have an advantage no other woman has. You're the mother of his children."

"Does he care for that?"

"Of course he does—and he will more, if you do. Show an interest and a pride in it, and you will be what no one else can be to him."

Mary thought, and seemed to see it. "Go on, go on!" She said, putting out her hand.

"Dear Mrs. Hillier, I have envied you so for that! All these years, I've never had that great happiness. At last"—she paused—"I'll tell you, if you care to know—at last, after ten years, I am going to have my wish."

"Really! And you are pleased?"

"I'm divinely happy, delighted!"

"Then I'm very glad for you, Mrs. Kellynch. But can't you imagine—you're so pretty and charming and good-tempered and clever. I'm none of all these things. I'm not pretty, and I'm very bad-tempered and terribly jealous by nature and not clever."

"You are his wife and he chose you. And he is a charming, pleasant man. You ought to be very happy together."

"To tell the truth—I don't mind what I tell you—I feel you're kind and good and sincere—I have always had a horrible feeling that he married me—because—because he was hard up. And I had money! And yet——"

"Oh, Mrs. Hillier, don't talk nonsense! It's dreadful of you to say so. You ought to be very glad to be able to have everything you want, without having to consider for your children. It's a great thing, I assure you, to have no money troubles. It's another very big reason for you and Nigel to be happy. You don't know what it is. It's agony! I do, because before I was married I was one of a very large family, and my father was a very popular preacher and all that, but it was a terrible struggle. To send the boys to public schools and Oxford, the girls had to be really dreadfully pinched! And always worries about bills! I was brought up in that atmosphere, and I know that to be entirely free from it is a most enormous relief and comfort. You will probably never know how fortunate you are."

"You are right. Of course Nigel is not the man to endure money troubles well."

"Exactly. Well, now, can't you see that you've every possible chance of happiness together?"

"May I call you Bertha?" answered Mary. "You've been a real angel to me, I might have expected you to refuse to see me, or at least to be cold and unkind—and instead you're as sorry as you can be for me and want to see me happy! You are sweet."

"Of course I'd like to see you happy," said Bertha. "You understand now that I also care for my husband? You're not the only one in the world, though I admit we're rather exceptions nowadays!"

"Yes; and I thought because you were so pretty and sweet that you *must* be a flirt—at the very least."

"I don't say I'm not, all the same. But I would never wish to interfere with other people's happiness."

"I sometimes think it might be better if *I* were a little of a flirt," sighed Mary. "But I can't—it's not my nature—or, rather, I'm too busy always looking after Nigel!"

"Well, don't do that so much and he'll look after you all the more. Show interest in your appearance and society—let him be proud of you—and *don't* be afraid of being fond of the children!"

"I'm really tremendously fond of them," said Mary. "Only I was always so afraid he would think they would do instead of him! I have such a horror of his sending me off with them and thinking they will fill up all my life, while he was living like a gay bachelor! And when he was very sweet to them I really was jealous of them!"

"But all this is absurd. If you show your affection for them he will love you far more, and when *he* is devoted to them it shows he's devoted to you. Don't be foolish, Mrs. Hillier, you have had a sort of crisis. Do let it end there. Let things be different. He will be delighted to see you cheerful and jolly again. It's all in your own hands, really."

"Thank you. It was a shame to bother you." She got up to go.

"May I tell you, later on . . . how things are? I shall follow your advice *exactly*!"

Mary was looking at her now in a kind of worshipping gratitude and trust.

"Yes, do. But I know it will be all right. Only be a little patient just now. . . . He will miss you awfully, I know," said Bertha, smiling.

"Oh! Will he *really*? How *sweet* of you to say that! Good-bye, Bertha. Dear Bertha, you have been kind. I'm *so* sorry." Tears came to her eyes again, but as she passed the little mirror she began to laugh. "To think I should have come to see you for the first time got up like a dame in a pantomime. How grotesque!"

They both laughed. Laughter altered and improved Mary wonderfully. It was a faculty she never exercised. She was always much too serious.

"Do you know, I haven't one woman friend," said Mary.

"Yes, you have, *now*." Bertha pressed her hand.

"Good-bye! . . . Oh, Bertha, do you *really* think he'll miss me?"

"Of course he will! Awfully!"

"Thanks. Good-bye!"

*

"Poor girl!" Bertha said to herself as Mary left the house.

CHAPTER XXXVI

PLAIN SAILING

WHETHER or not it was through meeting Nigel, at any rate, Rupert became exceedingly anxious to see Madeline again. It would have happened anyhow, but perhaps a little more slowly, since Nigel's rapid views may have had some influence on that more deliberate young man.

However that may be, in the early autumn Madeline, almost overcome with joy, was married to her adored and cultured instructor. She always remained his painstaking pupil; and he seemed highly gratified with her general progress; while she continued to be equally pleased with his mode of instruction and anxious not to neglect her education in any way.

When Nigel joined his wife he found her decidedly improved. Perhaps he really had missed the fact that he was of far more importance to her than to anyone else in the world. She never conquered her jealousy; but she learnt to conceal it, and thus to keep the peace; the children became gradually a source of mutual interest that was a real tie between them; in fact it grew in time into a positive hobby and a cause of so much pride and satisfaction as to be rather a bore to many of their friends.

I find I am finishing my story in a manner no less strange than unconventional nowadays: I am leaving no less than three almost perfectly happy couples! If this is a strain on the imagination of the reader, let it be remembered that they had all had their troubles and storms before they reached this point of smooth water.

Nigel, of course, deserved his peace and comfort the least. Percy, however, with his squash rackets and afternoon concerts (which, however, he grew to neglect in order to be more with Bertha), was the least interesting of all my heroes. Yet Bertha remained, I must admit, of all my heroines, by far the most in love.

CPSIA information can be obtained
at www.ICGtesting.com
Printed in the USA
BVHW082100070323
659869BV00001B/77